It was only a dream...

Drenched in perspiration, Dani struggled against labored breathing and the violent, uncontrollable trembling of her body. Apparently, she had woken herself up with the shrill sound of her own scream.

"Deep breaths," she whispered to herself.

The door to the bedroom burst open. The sheer size of the silhouetted figure identified him even before he'd flipped on the light. Tyler.

He wore nothing except for jeans, the top button left undone. His hair was mussed, probably disheveled from sleep. The hair that covered his chest tapered into a V before disappearing beneath his waistband.

"Are you all right?" he asked softly.

She nodded. "I had a bad dream," she said, wondering what he was doing in her room in the middle of the night. Half-dressed, no less.

She pulled the comforter up beneath her chin. His eyes eloquently conveyed his opinion of her action.

"You don't need to worry," he mocked. "My taste doesn't run to frightened women."

ABOUT THE AUTHOR

Kelsey Roberts lives with her husband, Bob, and son, Kyle, in Pasadena, Maryland. She is the coordinator for the writer's workshop at Anne Arundel Community College, and owns a custom matting business with her sister. But Kelsey devotes most of her time to the thrill of writing for Harlequin. In her free time, she enjoys traveling with her family.

Books by Kelsey Roberts

Don't miss any of our special offers. Write to us at the following address for information on our newest releases.

Harlequin Reader Service
U.S.: 3010 Walden Ave., P.O. Box 1325, Buffalo, NY 14269
Canadian: P.O. Box 609, Fort Erie, Ont. L2A 5X3

Things Remembered
Kelsey Roberts

Harlequin Books

TORONTO • NEW YORK • LONDON
AMSTERDAM • PARIS • SYDNEY • HAMBURG
STOCKHOLM • ATHENS • TOKYO • MILAN
MADRID • WARSAW • BUDAPEST • AUCKLAND

To Bob and Kyle, who gave me support;
To my sister Linda, who gave me encouragement;
And to Mom and Dad, who gave me a laptop!

ISBN 0-373-22294-7

THINGS REMEMBERED

Copyright © 1994 by Rhonda Pollero

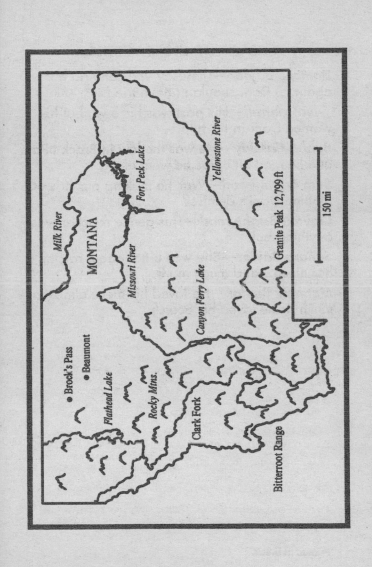

Brock's Pass
• Beaumont
Flathead Lake
Rocky Mtns.
Clark Fork
Bitterroot Range
Milk River
MONTANA
Missouri River
Fort Peck Lake
Canyon Ferry Lake
Yellowstone River
Granite Peak 12,799 ft
150 mi

CAST OF CHARACTERS

Danielle Baylor—They say you can't go home again.... Dani shouldn't have tried.

Tyler Cantrell—His past was his own, but he wanted Dani in his future.

Bubba Cassidy—He was the law in Brock's Pass and he made it up as he went along.

Sam Brightwood—Was he making amends or plotting Dani's demise?

Clayton Brightwood—This gentle rancher was anything but.

Sandra Baylor—She was bitter about raising her niece...and much more.

Matthew Baylor—He loved his niece almost as much as he loved his Scotch.

Chapter One

"What do you mean, *missing?*" Danielle Baylor screeched, clutching the front of the man's shirt.

Buck's expression lightened, and his faded blue eyes no longer held the hint of trepidation that had served as her initial warning flag. His rough hands came up and closed over hers as he spoke in a hushed, gravelly tone.

"Don't go all crazy now, Missy," the aged ranch hand said comfortingly. "You know as good as anybody that your sister's inclined to up and disappearing."

"Not for five days," Dani countered with a shake of her head. Releasing her grip, she ran her hands over the resulting wrinkles in his shirt as she looked around the interior of the small terminal. Several pairs of curious eyes were turned in her direction. Embarrassment caused a faint stain to burn her cheeks.

"Did Jen tell anyone she was leaving?" she asked, in a voice that quieted as control overcame shock.

Buck shook his head and shrugged his weary shoulders. She heard him expel his breath as he leaned down and collected the small bag she'd dropped upon hearing why her sister had failed to meet the plane.

"I'm sure she's just holed up in the mountains. Why, she's most likely taking pictures of some critter. Just lost track of time, is all."

While Dani admitted that was a possibility, she had serious doubts about her sister being so irresponsible as to miss meeting her flight. When she and Jennifer spoke by phone two weeks earlier, her sister had said she was looking forward to their visit. She had even hinted that she was planning some sort of surprise for Dani.

So why had Jen suddenly decided to go off into the mountains?

"Don't look so worried. Hell, she's probably back to the house right now, waiting on us to fetch you home." Buck tugged her in the direction of the baggage claim area. It was actually little more than a section of the terminal cordoned off with a length of velvet rope purchased at a discount when one of the town's movie theaters closed down.

The sound of a conveyer belt filtered into the room on a cool burst of air as an outside slot was opened. Her green eyes fixed on the opening while her brain pondered the situation. She could only hope Buck was right. Jennifer must have innocently gone off on one of her prolonged nature binges and simply lost track of the time.

A smile curved the corners of her mouth as she conjured up a mental picture of her older sister. About the only thing they shared was their last name. Beyond that, Dani and Jennifer were as different as two people could be. Jennifer was in her glory camped out on some deserted mountainside with nothing but the sound of the wind or the howl of an animal for company. Conversely, Dani loathed any outing more primitive than a night at a Holiday Inn.

"Those two are mine," she said to Buck, pointing to the expensive set of luggage that bore her monogram.

She was in the act of leaning forward to retrieve the first suitcase when a dark hand came out of nowhere and grasped the shiny handle of her bag. Her eyes fixed on the hand for a split second before traveling upward, over a well-defined, muscular arm encased in a faded plaid shirtsleeve. Continuing on, her eyes roamed the breadth of his chest, up over the vast expanse of his shoulders, and on to his face.

Her breath caught in her throat, and her expression must have registered the shock that had rendered her body suddenly paralyzed.

Hoisting the case off the belt, he set it down in the small space that separated them. Dani smiled her thanks to the handsome stranger, unable to find her voice.

If his sudden appearance caught her off guard, that was nothing compared to the openly hostile glint in his rich brown eyes.

"Missy, this here is Tyler Cantrell. Ty, Danielle Baylor."

He nodded, though it looked as if even that small display of civility were difficult for him.

"Ma'am..." he drawled. His eyes narrowed disapprovingly.

"Ty's our new foreman."

Dani's smile evolved into a more aloof expression as she tilted her head back in deference to his superior height. The way he was staring down his slightly crooked nose at her made her bristle. Something about the arrogant thrust of his marvelous cleft chin stiffened her spine. She had more pressing things on her mind than a large man with an even larger chip on his shoulder, even if that shoulder *was* the broadest she had ever seen.

"Mr. Cantrell," she returned frostily. Forcing her attention away from his face, she saw her other suitcase disappear behind a curtain of dusty, shredded fabric. *Great!* She fumed silently, knowing full well they would have to wait for the conveyer to make a second trip around.

A new and distracting scent raided her senses as she stood between the two men. It was fresh and hauntingly masculine. Dani knew it was *his*. That knowledge annoyed her almost as much as his inexplicable animosity. She could almost feel the contempt radiating from him, but she hadn't a clue as to its origins.

The conveyer belt jerked to a sudden, fatal halt. Dani rolled her eyes and let out a disgusted sigh. Murphy's Law had definitely followed her to Montana from Atlanta.

"Buck," she said, turning to the smaller man, "why don't we get the car? Mr. Cantrell can stand here and wait for the rest of my things."

Without waiting for a reply, Dani slipped her hand through Buck's arm and ushered him in the direction of the exit.

"It ain't fair to Ty to leave him there. No way of knowing when they'll get that thing running again."

"I know," Dani acknowledged with a devilish light in her emerald-colored eyes.

Buck seemed perplexed by her attitude. His forehead wrinkled into a series of deep crevasses. "Now, don't go getting the wrong idea, Missy. I know Tyler can be a mite standoffish, but—"

"Combative is more like it, Buck," Dani told him. "I don't like surly cowboys. Never have. You know that."

"Tyler isn't surly," Buck told her.

While she took issue with his assessment of the other man's character, Dani wasn't in the mood to argue the point. Aside from that, she knew once they got to the Circle B, Tyler would go his way and she hers. The ranch was big enough that, with any luck, they'd rarely cross paths during her stay.

Buck told her to stay by the entrance while he got the car from the lot. She waited at the curb, shivering against the cool evening air. According to the calendar, summer was just a few weeks off—a fact apparently lost on the frigid breeze whipping scraps of paper around her feet.

The area where she waited was deserted, except for a man standing a few yards away. His head was trapped in the folds of a road map.

She took a deep breath, savoring the taste and smell of the crisp, clean air. She smiled unconsciously as the scent brought back a flood of memories, some pleasant, some disastrous.

Her lashes fluttered closed against a sudden gust of wind that rustled the hem of the skirt. Automatically her hands moved to the fronts of her thighs in an attempt to keep her skirt from blowing to an immodest height.

"Doing a Marilyn Monroe impression?" a deep voice asked.

Hearing the derisive edge to his tone, she opted not to turn and look in the direction of the sound. Try as she might, Dani couldn't think of a single retort, so she stood stiffly at the curb and made a production of scanning the parking lot for some sign of Buck.

"Construction," he said after a brief, tense silence. "The lot's being renovated. Waste of good tax dollars, if you ask me."

She thought about the archaic terminal and doubted that any improvement could be construed as a waste. The airport hadn't been changed by so much as the color of the paint for more than twenty years. She was going to tell him exactly that, but when she turned and saw his profile, the words stuck in her constricted throat.

His Stetson, which was a pale shade of gray, was pulled low over his forehead. It accentuated both the size and intensity of his dark eyes. In the low light, they appeared very nearly black, edged in long, thick lashes. She swallowed as her eyes surveyed the unyielding set of his mouth. Disdain appeared to radiate from every inch of his handsome face.

She had been so engrossed in her moonlit perusal of him that she started when the piercing sound of a horn exploded next to her.

Her heart fell to her toes when she spied the pickup. It meant she would have to suffer through thirty miles of Tyler's surly attitude inside the small confines of the utility vehicle.

Buck came around from the driver's side and assisted Tyler in securing her bags in a compartment in the truck's bed. Dani looked nervously inside the cab. The bench seat seemed small and inadequate for a man of Tyler's height and breadth.

She was right. A few seconds later she found herself sandwiched between the two men.

"Sure is good to have you home, Missy," Buck said.

Grinning at his kind sentiment, she chose to ignore the disgusted snort from the man to her right. Just as she chose to ignore the heat from his thigh, where it rubbed against hers. And just as she chose to ignore the solidness of his body whenever Buck negotiated a turn and the centrifugal forces molded her against him.

She could not, however, ignore the musky, masculine scent of his cologne, not when it teased her senses. Nor could she ignore the way her body seemed to be reacting to this man.

"Comfortable?" Tyler spoke the taunt against her ear. His breath was warm where it washed over the sensitive skin of her neck.

"Delightfully," she returned sweetly, fighting the urge to reach up and wipe away the tingling feeling at the side of her throat. She shifted closer toward Buck, silently reminding herself that she was a perfectly normal woman, not some sort of sex-starved spinster.

"How long's it been?" Buck asked.

Dani choked on her own saliva. Buck attempted to drive and pat her on the back at the same time. It didn't work, not in the small confines of the passenger compartment. Leaning forward, she struggled to contain the coughing and the tears that were her biological punishment for self-induced choking.

The feel of a large hand at the center of her back had a miraculous effect. His fingers seared through the fabric of her blouse, leaving a fiery imprint just between her shoulder blades. Patting gently, Tyler soothed the spastic muscles in her body long enough to allow Dani to regain her composure.

She was grateful it was too shadowy for him to see her face clearly. Her cheeks were damp from the tears, and she felt herself blushing with total humiliation from the roots of her hair all the way down to her feet.

"You okay?" Buck asked, his voice soft with concern.

"Fine," she whispered. She retrieved a tissue from her purse and dabbed at her eyes.

Tyler unhurriedly slid his hand away from her back, allowing his fingertips to linger a fraction of a second longer than necessary.

Suddenly one of the truck's tires found a deep rut in the highway, tossing Dani about the cabin and bouncing her even closer to Tyler.

"Would you like to sit on my lap?" he asked softly.

"If you're uncomfortable, you can always ride in the back," she said to him with a forced smile. Dani shifted herself so that her body touched as little of his as possible.

Buck appeared to notice the wall of tension separating his passengers. "Now don't go biting at Ty. I know you're worried about Jen. But like I told you, I'm sure she's remembered herself and she's waiting up to the house."

"I hope you're right," she mused softly. "Has anyone gone out looking for her?"

She watched as Buck bobbed his head. "Ty spent most of the day out and about, trying to track her down."

Dani turned and met the full force of Tyler's eyes. "Did you find any sign of her? A campsite? Anything?"

He nodded slowly. The strands of blond hair framing his face caught the light. "Found several places where she's been the past few days."

"Was anything out of the ordinary?"

He watched Dani's forehead wrinkle. It was obvious she was holding out hope for something that might explain her sister's sudden disappearance.

Tyler was fascinated by the emotions playing across her face. The depth of her concern piqued his interest.

Shrugging his shoulder against hers, he said, "Nothing that would indicate anything out of the ordinary."

She didn't challenge his answer. Dani was nothing like her sister. He was certain of that. This one was more controlled. Yet he sensed the control was hard won. He had the feeling she was somehow vulnerable. That realization only made him feel worse.

"You went and choked yourself half to death before you answered my question, Missy. How long's it been since your last visit?" Buck asked.

He heard her let out a slow breath before responding. "Nearly two years," she answered finally.

Buck whistled. Tyler placed one large hand on his knee and began to tap out a rhythm against his jeans. He was trying not to notice the feminine scent that clung to the silky strands of hair framing her face. Just as he was trying not to notice the perfect shape of her incredible body.

"I knew it had been a while. I'm surprised you let so much time pass. Why, when you were a little girl, you used to swear you'd never go no farther from the Circle B than the back fence."

Her expression seemed to soften, lingering somewhere between sadness and amusement. "I'm not a little girl anymore, Buck."

Tyler's thumb stilled at her words, his eyes taking in her profile in the flash of oncoming headlights. He noted that she held in her breath. She must have been acutely aware of his eyes roaming over her face before traveling lower to take in the silhouette of her body through the thin silk blouse that outlined every feminine inch of her, including the wispy lace at the edge of her brassiere.

The expression in her eyes caused a tight knot to form in the pit of his stomach. He felt guilty about the sadness, but was impressed by the twinkle of amusement. Danielle was the most intriguing woman he'd encountered in some time. Certainly the most intriguing he'd encountered in Brock's Pass.

He could see by the vibration of the tiny vein at the base of her slender throat that her pulse quickened under his blatant scrutiny. His base instincts kicked in, and he swallowed his smile. Deliberately Tyler shifted in his seat, brushing his leg against hers. She edged closer to Buck. Next he pretended to scratch his chin, but his real goal was to feel the soft material of her blouse. He liked watching her cool exterior melt. He especially liked the way any intimate contact knocked her off-balance. It was a bit of knowledge he decided to store for future use.

A FEELING washed over Dani, something vague and indefinable, but nonetheless disturbing. Taking her lead from Buck and Tyler, she pushed any and all negative thoughts from her brain. Dani comforted herself with the knowledge that they had only a short distance left to travel. She could hardly wait to see her sister, and she'd had quite enough of Tyler—and those eyes the color of expensive imported chocolate.

The road surface became noticeably worse when they turned onto the stone drive that led up to the house. Still, Dani was grateful that this endurance test was about to come to an end.

For the last five or so miles of the trip, she could have sworn Tyler had gone out of his way to make her as uncomfortable as possible. If he wasn't rubbing his leg against hers, then he was lifting an arm, brushing his tight, sinewy muscles against her until she was forced to squirm and wiggle in the seat to maintain distance.

The moon slipped behind the house, outlining the two-story home that dominated a large portion of the landscape. The weathered log exterior and full porch were bathed in lights that began over the front door and continued in a semicircle around the front lawn. The floodlights only added to the majestic feel of the place.

Dani's sense of excitement rose as she waited for Tyler to exit the vehicle. Once he no longer served as an impediment to her progress, she bounded from the truck and up the stairs, taking them two at a time. The buttery scent of baking greeted her just a second before her hand closed on the cool metal doorknob. Pushing the door open, she was welcomed by two smiling faces. The third face in the hallway looked just as sour and unfriendly as ever.

"Aunt Sandra." She acknowledged the stiff, unpleasant woman first, in order to get it over with.

"Lupe!" Dani exclaimed with genuine enthusiasm. Moving forward, she wrapped her arms as far around the woman as Lupe's girth would allow.

"Look at you!" Lupe countered, using the corner of her apron to dab at a tear in the crease beside one brown eye. "If you aren't the image of your mama." The woman shook her head and rested her hands against her ample hips.

"Do you have a hug for your favorite uncle?" a male voice chimed.

Matthew rushed forward, placing a fatherly kiss on her forehead and giving a gentle squeeze where his hands clutched her upper arms.

"Of course I do," Dani said, pulling the distinguished man to her. His affection was genuine, and very comforting.

They held each other at arm's length for a brief time before her uncle spoke again. "Danielle, you get prettier with each passing year."

She smiled up at him, amazed by the changes apparent since last they'd been together. It seemed as though during the course of her long absence Uncle Matt had aged ten years. Dani sneaked a peek at her aunt and decided Sandra was basically the same. Still attractive, still cool, still aloof, and still Dani's least favorite person on earth.

"Has there been any word from Jennifer?" she asked as she locked arms with her uncle and they proceeded in the direction of the spacious kitchen.

Uncle Matt, along with everyone else, seemed totally unconcerned by Jennifer's disappearance. Shrugging his shoulders, her uncle led her through the richly paneled hallway.

The kitchen was a long room, decorated with many of the rustic utensils and hand-carved implements owned and used by the Baylor family when they had first settled the land, more than a century earlier. Dani's great-great-grandfather had made his way through the territories to western Montana and had personally staked out what was now the Circle B Ranch. The house had changed over time, with additions made to accommodate children, then again to accommodate modern conveniences, then, finally, to accommodate luxury. It was something of a showplace, and starkly different from her humble, though functional, condominium back in Atlanta.

Seated at the large oak table that dominated the room, Dani tried to keep her worries at bay. Still, her eyes went to the huge window and looked out at the unforgiving, moonlit landscape beyond.

Aunt Sandra glided into the chair opposite Dani and clasped her hands in front of her on the table. To Dani, she looked bored, but still somehow managed to silently convey the fact that she was less than pleased with Dani's appearance at the ranch. The fact that Dani and her sister each owned forty-five percent of the ranch was conveniently ignored by her aunt. Sandra lorded over the place like royalty.

"How's the thesis coming?" Matt asked as Lupe placed a tray of steaming coffee mugs at the center of the round table.

"Slowly," she admitted. "I've finished all my research. Now it's just a matter of pulling everything together into a coherent presentation."

"What is it you hope to accomplish with this thing?" Sandra interjected.

"Earning my PhD," she responded, in a flat tone that matched her aunt's.

Tyler sauntered into the kitchen. Dani was surprised to see that he apparently had free run of the house. The practice of allowing the ranch hands access to the house had ended with the tragedy, more than twenty years earlier.

Dumbfounded, she watched as Tyler made his way over to the tray and helped himself to a cup of coffee. Next, he turned one of the chairs backward, scraping the legs noisily across the floor, and mounted it. Removing his hat and hanging it on the chair, Tyler gave Lupe a playful wink before taking a sip from his cup.

"We appreciate you going with Buck to collect Dani," Matt said. "I'm sure he welcomed the help."

"No problem," Tyler responded smoothly. His voice, when not tainted by sarcasm, was rich, deep, and utterly sexy.

Dani looked down into her mug, for fear her expression might reveal the carnal nature of her thoughts. *Fatigue,* she told herself. She was exhausted from the time change, and that explained her reaction to a man who openly, and for no apparent reason, disliked her.

"Is she just worried about Jennifer, or is she always this quiet?" Tyler asked as Lupe placed a freshly baked fruit pie on the table, followed by the requisite number of plates and forks.

"I *am* worried about my sister, Mr. Cantrell." Dani stressed her words through thinned lips. "It isn't like Jen to not meet me. We're very close."

"Is that why you haven't been back to visit in two years?"

Dani stiffened in response to the question. While everyone at the table exchanged shocked looks, Dani stared hard at the man.

"Mr. Cantrell," she began, in a deceptively calm voice, "is there something about me that bothers you, or are you always this obnoxious?"

His eyes met and held hers. Gold sparks emanated from the light reflecting in his pupils. His jaw thrust forward, and his chest rose and fell with each breath.

She noted that his large fingers gripped the mug just a bit too tightly.

"Danielle—" her aunt's voice cut through threads of tension weaving between Dani and the cowboy "—would you please try and refrain from causing any unpleasantness? I'm sure Tyler didn't mean anything by his comment. And you must admit that you've taken very little interest in this place, or any of *us,* since you went off to college."

Dani turned her attention to the woman who had acted, albeit unwillingly, as a surrogate mother since the time of her parents' tragic death. "We've been over this before, Aunt Sandra. I don't see what there is for me to do here. Uncle Matt manages the business aspects. You seem to have a handle on the household, as well as all the charity matters. I don't see what I have to contribute."

"Your sister certainly doesn't think like that," Sandra countered in a tone that implied that Dani would always be inferior to her sibling.

"No, she doesn't," Dani agreed quickly. Glancing down at her watch, she acknowledged a new world record in Baylor family discord—she and her aunt had exchanged harsh words during the first ten minutes. As was par for the course, Lupe and Uncle Matt leaned back in their chairs and pretended not to notice the friction between the two women.

The behavior was part of a ritual that had begun at some point during Dani's seventh year of life. That was the year Dani had first challenged Sandra's authority, and this ritual continued throughout the years. The other members of the household tried simply to ignore the spats. It was safer than taking one side over the other—especially for Uncle Matt. While he adored his nieces, he was the one who suffered the wrath of Sandra whenever he dared to side with Dani or Jennifer. In the end, it had become easier for him just to feign deafness.

Dani took a deep breath and shifted in her seat.

Lupe's round face contorted into a mass of exasperated frustration. Uncle Matt's expression was more disappointed than anything else. But it was Tyler's expression that riled Dani.

Leaning forward, resting his forearms against the chair back, Tyler appeared to be enjoying the volley of verbal lashes. His lips turned up slightly at one corner, forming something dangerously close to a satisfied smirk. With his blond head tilted to one side, his eyes brimmed with unspoken challenge. It was obvious that he would have derived great pleasure from having Dani and her aunt air all the dirty family laundry as his evening entertainment.

Refusing to rise to the bait, and in the interest of maintaining some sort of personal dignity, Dani forced herself to smile at the arrogant man. "My aunt is right, Mr. Cantrell. I apologize if you felt I was rude to you."

A flicker of disappointment flashed in the depths of his dark eyes before being replaced by a more utilitarian expression. His head dipped fractionally, as if her hard-won self-control had actually scored a point with the argumentative creature.

Not that I care, she told herself as she absently reached for a generous slice of pie. Dani wondered what it was about the light-haired cowboy that had her second-guessing her every word and deed.

A period of silence followed as everyone enjoyed the pie. Dani found herself alternately peering out the window for some sign of Jennifer's return and fighting the urge to stare openly at Tyler. She might not care much for his attitude, but Dani was forced to acknowledge to herself that he was one very attractive man. With the exception of his hair, everything about him was dark and rather mysterious-looking. Each feature, excluding his nose, looked as if it had been lovingly sculpted to perfection. She suspected the slight misalignment of his nose was the result of some injury gone untreated. A broken nose wasn't an uncommon thing. Over the years, Dani had encountered many men working at the ranch who had suffered the same fate at least a time or two. But instead of leaving the usual unsightly bump, the slight imperfection only served to enhance Tyler's vastly masculine appearance.

"I'm sorry," Dani said after hiding a yawn behind her napkin. "I think Lupe's delicious pie has lulled me into a state of utter contentment."

"I know what you mean," Uncle Matt agreed, patting the flabby distension of his stomach where it protruded over the waistband of his jeans. "I always sleep better on a full stomach."

"Your stomach's always full," Sandra pointed out, her obvious censure apparent as she gazed upon her husband's rounded midriff.

"True," Matt countered, heedless of his wife's displeasure.

Dani shook her head, suddenly remembering why she had allowed so much time to lapse between visits. The Circle B wasn't home—it was a battleground! At least it seemed that way without Jennifer there to act as a buffer between the various warring factions.

"Did Jennifer tell any of you that she was planning a trip into the mountains?" Dani asked no one in particular.

"No."

"Nope."

"No. And you'd better believe she'll hear about that, too," Lupe said, waving her wooden spoon in the air. "That girl ought to have more sense than to take off, when she knew good and well you were due in today."

"It's not like her," Dani readily agreed.

"It sure isn't, but that girl's been acting strange as all get-out lately."

Dani gaped at Lupe, unaccustomed to hearing the housekeeper utter anything that wasn't totally complimentary toward a Baylor girl. Her light brows arched in surprise. "What do you mean, *strange?*"

"Strange," Lupe repeated, as if that were explanation enough. "Your sister's mind has been off somewhere her body just wasn't."

Running one artfully manicured fingernail around the rim of her coffee cup, Dani stared down into the empty vessel. All sorts of frightening thoughts entered her head, and she felt a rush of trepidation well up inside her. "Have any of you considered calling the authorities?"

Sandra dismissed the comment with a wave of her hand. Uncle Matt turned the handle of an engraved spoon between his thumb and forefinger, staring at it intently, as if actually contemplating the idea. Lupe nodded instant agreement. Tyler only stared at her, his face devoid of any discernible thought or emotion.

"If Jen's been out there for five days without radioing in, anything might have happened to her—" Dani's voice cracked at the end of the statement, as if stating the very real possibility that something awful had happened could somehow make it a reality.

"Don't be such an alarmist, Danielle," Sandra instructed. "Your sister is completely capable of taking care of herself. Why, Jennifer is one of the most cautious, level-headed people I know. I'm sure she's just lost track of the time. If you call the sheriff's department, you'll only embarrass this family...*again*."

Dani's cheeks burned with a mixture of anger and discomfiture. Mentally she tried to calculate just how long her aunt could continue throwing the past in her face. Sandra was twenty years Dani's senior, which meant that, if they both lived to the national average of about seventy-six, Dani could count on having that unfortunate incident flung in her face for approximately thirty more years. It was a grim thought. The whole thing had been Sam's fault—no matter what Sheriff Cassidy and his band of bozos thought.

"No, Aunt Sandra. I was just suggesting that *something* should be done. After all, Jen might be hurt..."

"Tyler's been up the mountain. He found a few campsites. No one's reported seeing any flares or signal fires," Matt said.

Somehow her uncle's speech failed to completely eradicate the unpleasant thoughts milling around in Dani's brain.

She rose, carefully sidestepped Tyler, and placed her soiled dishes in the sink. "I'm exhausted from the trip," she admitted. "I think I'll call it a night."

"I'm a bit tuckered out myself," Matt chorused.

She felt a pair of brown eyes boring into her back as she exited the kitchen.

RAIN POUNDED *against the windowpane, rattling the glass in harmony with the wind, which was howling like a big scary animal. Dani's eyes remained open, staring past the darkness to the silhouettes of her dolls and toys. Their lifeless eyes sparkled each time a white bolt of lightning flashed through the room. She knew it was silly to be scared. After all, she'd just turned six, and six-year-olds were too big to be scared of the dark.*

Dani hugged Scruffy against her flannel gown as her ears picked up the muffled sounds of voices wafting up from below. Clutching the pilled toy more tightly, she closed her eyes and tried to ignore the rain, the darkness and the angry voices growing louder with each passing second.

"I wish Mommy and Daddy wouldn't fight," she whispered to the bear. The crash of yet another round of thunder jolted her into a sitting position. Forgetting the fact that she was sure to get her fanny swatted, Dani scooted off the bed and padded toward the

door. The knob was high and hard to turn, so she had to put Scruffy on the floor and use both hands. She heard a popping sound just as the door creaked open and bright light blinded her. Rubbing her eyes to get rid of those funny red spots, Dani collected her bear and dragged him silently behind her as she moved down the long hall as quietly as she could. Her fingers trailed along the surface of the wall. It felt cool and smooth as she made her way down the corridor.

At the top of the stairs, her heart sang when the angry voices suddenly grew still. If they weren't fighting, maybe they wouldn't spank her for getting out of bed.

The bear's legs thumped against the tread as she carefully took each steep step. She smelled something funny, and crinkled her nose in response. It smelled a little like the fires they built out by the holding pens. Dani wondered if you could brand cattle indoors. Maybe, if it was raining really hard, like now.

At the bottom of the stairs, she nearly lost her balance on the polished wood floor. Skidding into the corner, she could see directly into the shadowy living room. Daddy was laying on the sofa, one leg bent under his body. He looked a little like the woman Dani had seen at the circus—the one who could tie herself up like a pretzel. Mommy was there, too, sitting very still. It wasn't like Mommy to sit still.

A sudden flash of lightning illuminated the room. There was a large boo-boo on daddy's head, just below where his hair met his forehead. Something dark and reddish was running from his fingertips into a puddle on the floor.

Panic welled up in her body. Frozen, she pressed herself tightly against the wall and waited for the next flash of lightning. When it came, she clearly saw a black-handled knife. Dani's breath caught when she sensed someone moving inside the room.

There was another flash, but it wasn't from the storm outside. It was quick and filled the air around her with more of that stinky, smoky smell. With the next jolt of lightning, Dani stared dumbstruck at the scene before her. Daddy's boo-boo was worse, and yucky stuff seemed to be splattered everywhere. Dani opened her mouth to scream just as she saw—

Chapter Two

Dani sat bolt upright in the bed. Drenched in perspiration, she found herself struggling against labored breathing and the violent, uncontrollable trembling of her body. Apparently, she had woken herself up with the shrill sound of her own scream.

"Deep breaths," she whispered to herself.

The door to the room burst open. The sheer size of the silhouetted figure identified him even before he reached around and flipped the switch to flood the room with light.

Instinctively holding the sheets to her chest, Dani sucked in deep breaths as he took the two long strides necessary to reach her bedside. He wore nothing except his jeans. The button at the top of the waistband had been left undone. His hair was mussed, probably disheveled from sleep.

He stood next to the bed, apparently trying to decide what to do next. Ignoring the awkwardness of the situation, Dani focused on an unobstructed view of the dark mat of hair that covered his chest, then tapered into a V before disappearing into his jeans.

"Are you all right?" he asked softly.

She nodded, feeling like every kind of fool known to mankind. "I had a bad dream," she said, wondering why on earth she should be explaining herself to him. For that matter, what was he doing in her room in the middle of the night? Half-dressed, no less.

She pulled the comforter to a spot just beneath her chin. His eyes eloquently conveyed his opinion of her action.

"You don't need to worry. My taste doesn't run to frightened women."

Her lips parted with the anticipation of a retort—one her frazzled brain failed to supply. In any event, Tyler wasn't quite finished.

She made the fatal mistake of looking directly into the frosty brown depths of his eyes. They narrowed with open contempt as he surveyed the traces of dampness sheening the pale skin of her forehead.

"The only reason I set foot in this room was because I heard you screaming like a banshee. Otherwise, the proverbial wild horses wouldn't have been able to drag me in here."

He stood glaring at her, and she felt her face grow warm, as if his eyes possessed the power to ignite a fire on their own. Lowering her gaze, Dani took in the sight of his broad chest, gently rising and falling with each breath. It was only mildly less distracting than his handsome face.

"I apologize for disturbing your sleep, Mr. Cantrell," she informed him flatly.

Reaching out, he captured her chin between the rough tips of his thumb and forefinger and exerted just enough pressure to force eye contact. Stiffly, Dani allowed him to raise her face. Tyler leaned closer, close enough for his breath to caress her face. Her pulse quickened involuntarily as his eyes dropped to the edge of the blanket she clutched modestly against herself. "You don't need to do that, Danielle. *Trust* me, I'm not interested."

"Then why are you still in here?" she returned.

"Trust *me,* it's not because I want *you* in my room."

She hadn't thought it was possible to stomp from a room in bare feet—she was wrong. The sound of Tyler's exit echoed in her brain long after he'd gone.

"Don't give it a thought, Cantrell," she muttered to the closed door, and slipped off the high bed. "I'll get up and turn out the light."

Once back in bed, Dani lay there wondering in the darkened solitude of her room. *What was Tyler doing in the house?* To her recollection, the ranch hands were not usually permitted to take up residence in the main house. There was a trailer at the edge of the property supplied to the foreman as a perk. She could only assume that Aunt Sandra must have invited him to stay the night.

And where are you, Jennifer? Rolling onto her side, Dani punched down the pillow. Jennifer could be something of a free spirit, but she was normally a responsible free spirit. It was only after Dani had reassured herself that her sister would definitely appear in the morning that she was able to fall back to sleep.

THANKS to an internal clock set on East Coast time, Dani rose before the rest of the household. From the closet adjoining her room, she selected a pair of jeans and an olive-colored sweater from among the offerings. On one of her trips west, she would eventually get around to cleaning out her closets. She might as well donate the contents. It seemed such a waste to hang on to these things when she so rarely visited.

Her hand reached out and stroked a formal gown constructed of brilliant forest green sequins sewn onto smooth silk. A wry smile touched her lips as she remembered the one and only time she'd worn that dress. She and Jennifer had driven hundreds of miles during the weeks preceding the dance, searching for just the right dress for Dani's special evening. They'd gone to Beaumont, then back to Brock's Pass, then back to Beaumont and home again, before they discovered the strapless creation in a small boutique in Brock's Pass proper. Dani had purchased it on the spot. Sandra had been furious when they arrived home with the dress.

"That night was the beginning of the end," she said before turning on her heel and exiting the spacious walk-in closet. Sandra had probably purposely hung the dress in an obvious spot, just in case Dani dared to forget.

Securing her hair at the nape of her neck with a carved silver barrette, Dani pulled on socks and boots, then slipped noiselessly from the room.

Lupe had thoughtfully set up the coffeepot so that all Dani had to do was flip a switch and exercise eight minutes of patience.

Seated at the table, she watched as a slowly rising sun painted the landscape outside the picture window a brilliant shade of gold. The mountain range that edged the western portion of the ranch seemed even more imposing in the first light of day.

She had that distant look in her eyes. The one that had him teetering between wanting to protect her and wanting to kiss the breath out of her. He wasn't quite sure what was happening to him. Danielle was not what he had expected, and certainly not something he was prepared for. Still, he was too far in to back out now. With all the bravado he could muster, Tyler walked into the room.

"I wouldn't have pegged you as an early riser."

Dani jumped at his voice. He felt her eyes on him as he pulled a mug from the cabinet.

He watched as she tried to assume an air of aloofness. He'd seen it the previous night, when she'd looked at him as though he were some pillaging pirate come to ravage her. Apparently her task was complicated when she noticed he had neglected to button the front of his shirt. He watched with some measure of pure male pride as she struggled to keep from gaping at his body. He had the sinking suspicion that Dani wasn't all that comfortable in the company of a half-dressed man. He liked that.

The coffeepot sputtered a few times, then grew quiet. Tyler poured some for himself and joined her at the table. He left a trail of sugar when he added the sweetener to his cup. He hoped she wouldn't notice.

Suddenly her pretty features hardened and her green eyes narrowed. It was only then that he realized that he hadn't bothered to offer to get her a cup. He was about to jump up when she got up to fill her cup. Smooth, Tyler, he thought with disgust. Very smooth.

Dani went to the refrigerator, muttering something about cream. The appliance was well stocked, so it took her a minute to find the small carton wedged behind several bottles of unsweetened grape juice. The grape juice served as a hurtful reminder of Jennifer's absence. Jennifer started, sustained and ended every day of her life with a dreadful mixture of freshly brewed tea and unsweetened grape juice.

"Dilutes the purpose of the coffee," he observed as she poured a modest amount of cream into her mug.

He wore the same jeans as the night before, though she noted that the button was now secured and hidden beneath a large oval belt buckle. His torso and legs were wrapped in soft leather chaps, which only served to accentuate the power and definition of his thighs. Seated at the table, a mug dangling between two slightly squared fingers, Tyler regarded her with what she assumed was disinterest in his dark eyes.

"Tell me something, Mr. Cantrell," Dani began in a soft, intentionally feminine voice, then turned her back to him. "Will you be subjecting me to your opinions throughout my stay? Or is this morning just a special occasion?"

He cocked his head to one side, but he said nothing until she returned to her seat at the table. "Are you always so testy, Danielle?" He used her name as if it were some sort of curse that left a sour taste in his mouth.

"I am not testy. I was merely inquiring about your apparent penchant for finding fault with everything I do."

Her statement appeared to amuse him. The faint flicker of laughter glistening in his eyes inspired a sudden and fierce need in her to be on the defensive. Dani felt as if she were being toyed with by a master. It wasn't a particularly pleasant way to begin a day.

"Are you sure my observation about putting cream in your coffee is what's bothering you?"

"Of course!" she answered, giving him a disgusted look.

He threw his head back and laughed at her indignation.

Dani glared at him through narrowed eyes. She wasn't going to put up with being insulted by some hired hand.

As she squared her slender shoulders, Dani's rigid posture told him she wasn't the least bit amused by his attitude. His laughter subsided under the censure of her expression.

Tyler raised the mug to his chiseled mouth and took a sip. Dani tried not to acknowledge the part of her that seemed to fixate on his every move. After all, Tyler was the personification of everything she despised in a man. He was a bit too macho, a bit too uncivilized . . . and far too damned attractive.

Pushing that last thought from her head, she found her attention drawn back to the scene beyond the window. "What is Jennifer doing out there?"

"Probably taking a few pictures."

It wasn't until he answered that Dani realized she had voiced the question aloud.

"I don't think you have anything to worry about. Jen's a capable lady."

Instantly the obvious admiration in his tone captured her full attention. His demeanor, coupled with the genuine fondness with which he spoke of Jennifer, gave Dani cause to wonder if perhaps there was something personal between the two. Guilt tainted the curiosity. Had she been having carnal thoughts about a man who was involved with her own sister?

"What's wrong?"

Her head whipped around in response to the question. "What? I mean, nothing!"

"Then why the frown?"

"Was I frowning?" she asked innocently.

Tyler's head tilted to one side as he reached into the breast pocket of his shirt and removed a pack of cigarettes. Shaking one free, he rolled the filter across his tongue before securing it between his lips.

Dani's pulse reacted to the purely sensual action. Her brain still refused to admit that she found his movements appealing in a primal, unrefined sort of way.

The end of the cigarette glowed a deep amber where he had positioned the flame from a silver-and-turquoise lighter. The air between them quickly filled with the heady scent of soap, leather and smoke.

Dani fairly jumped from her seat and ran toward the coffeepot under the pretext of a refill on the coffee. Anything was better than sitting there. Watching him.

Get a grip! her brain screamed as she mechanically moved about the room. She was acting like a complete idiot, and all over some stuck-on-himself cowboy. Maybe the increase in altitude had affected her brain.

"Did you have any trouble getting back to sleep last night?"

She shook her head, wondering at the abrupt change in his tone. She no longer detected a veil of sarcasm draped over every syllable. Returning to the table, she sat and hugged the warm mug between both of her hands. Peering up through her lashes, she was almost sorry to see him temper his hostilities. His handsome features, punctuated by the most devilishly attractive half smile she'd ever seen, were very nearly irresistible. *Remember,* she cautioned herself, *he's a cowboy!*

"It took me a while to get back to sleep," she told him, glad that the words came out in a clear and steady voice.

"Because of the dream?"

A shiver ran the full length of her spine as she recalled the gruesome, vivid details. "No," she told him, wondering why, after so much time, the nightmare had returned.

He regarded her with an expression of anticipation. His brown eyes moved over her face, making her regret the fact that she had not exercised the extra effort to apply makeup.

"What was your dream about?"

Shrugging her shoulders, Dani pretended to dismiss the horrible nightmare as unimportant.

Still Tyler persisted. "You seemed pretty shook up when I came into your room."

"It was nothing," she insisted. "Really."

"Do you always break out in a sweat when you're dreaming about nothing?"

Her eyebrows drew together as she read the determined set of his jaw. "What difference does it make to you? It was only a bad dream. Every night, I'm sure, millions of Americans have bad dreams. It's no big deal."

"I think it is a big deal," he told her, with an incredible air of superiority.

"Well, you're wrong."

He leaned forward so that mere inches separated them. "Then would you mind telling me what a twenty-six-year-old graduate student is doing waking up in the middle of the night screaming for her mommy?"

Dani's heart skipped a beat, and a chill settled over her as she looked deep into those inquisitive brown eyes. "I called for my mother?"

"Yes," he said, in a soft, comforting tone that hinted there might be more to him than swaggering hips, broad shoulders and dazzling arrogance.

Shaking her head, Dani attempted to push all awareness of the man from her brain. "It was no big deal," she repeated, and diverted her eyes from his. "In fact, I can't really recall the exact details."

"You seem mighty upset right now for someone who can't remember details."

"Well, I can't," she told him, more forcefully.

He got up from the table to get a second cup of coffee. The sound of his bootheels against the tile floor echoed in the early morning silence of the house.

"You know," Tyler began, before turning to face her as he leaned against the countertop, "it might help you to talk about your nightmares. Maybe if you shared what it is that frightens you, it would go away."

Dani shook her head. "Excuse me?"

He smiled understandingly at her befuddled expression. "Sometimes talking things out makes them easier to deal with."

"I don't have anything to *deal* with!" Dani countered indignantly. "And how did we get on the inane subject of my nightmares in the first place?"

Placing his mug on the counter, Tyler raised his hands in mock surrender. The action caused the gap at the front of his shirt to widen, exposing even more of his broad chest and rippling stomach muscles. Dani struggled to remain focused on the matter at hand.

"I don't think recurrent nightmares are an inane subject."

"Who said anything about recurrent?" she demanded, fully expecting to hear yet another unflattering tale told by her bitter prune of an aunt.

"Jennifer."

"Jennifer?" she repeated, utterly shocked. "I don't believe you," she added firmly.

He shrugged his shoulders before bracing one hand on either side of his body. "Jennifer told me that you've been plagued with these nightmares for years. Ever since your parents died."

"Why?"

"Why what?"

"Why would you and my sister be discussing me?"

"She's worried about you. She thinks—"

"I know what Jennifer thinks," Dani said, cutting in. "She's wrong."

"Is she?"

"Yes," Dani hissed. "There's nothing to this dream. No basis in fact. Believe me, Mr. Cantrell, Jennifer went back and checked with Singletary's, the funeral home. My mother wasn't shot, she was stabbed, just like my father."

"Jennifer doesn't—"

"Speaking of my sister," Dani said, interrupting him again, "I'm really concerned about her. This isn't like her at all. I meant what I said last night. If she doesn't show up today, I'm calling the sheriff's department. I don't care what Aunt Sandra thinks."

"When did you ever care what I thought, Danielle?" Sandra, draped in some chiffon robe that billowed around her body like a personal cloud, floated into the room. Her auburn hair was twisted into a severe chignon at the nape of her long neck. Her thickly lashed blue eyes homed in on Dani, blazing with long-checked fury.

Taking a deep breath, Dani regretted the fact that her aunt had heard the latter portion of the conversation. "I didn't mean it like that," she said, in an attempt to smooth things over. "It's just that I'm very concerned about Jennifer. I'm sure none of us would ever be able to forgive ourselves if something happened to her while we sat around doing absolutely nothing."

Sandra moved over so that she was next to Tyler. For a brief instant, Dani could have sworn something clouded his expression. A private, secretive thought. Whatever it was—or possibly wasn't—didn't matter, because it vanished before Dani could get an accurate read.

"Danielle may be right," Tyler said, without much conviction.

"Would both of you stop this?" Sandra snapped. "Jennifer knows every inch of those mountains. She's neither careless nor stupid." She turned her eyes directly on Dani. "As usual, Danielle, you're imagining disaster where none exists."

"I suppose," she said, relenting after briefly reminding herself that her aunt's comments regarding Jennifer were accurate.

"I'm sure Jennifer will turn up at some point during the day. She knows we've invited the Brightwoods for dinner," Sandra said.

Dani nearly groaned aloud.

"Don't look like that!" her aunt said, referring to the grim expression that Dani never bothered to conceal.

"I'm sorry, Aunt Sandra. But I can't believe you would be so insensitive as to invite the Brightwoods here for dinner. You know how I feel!"

Tyler, who had been all but ignoring the two women, took a sudden interest in the conversation. "You aren't an admirer of Clayton Brightwood? I thought that was a prerequisite for living in Brock's Pass."

"Be quiet, Tyler." Sandra chided him as if he were no more than a small boy. "I don't want you to encourage Danielle's rudeness."

"Rudeness? When was I ever rude to Mr. Brightwood?"

"You are incessantly rude to him. Clayton Brightwood is a powerful man. The kind of man one should have as a friend—not an enemy."

"The man is a jerk," Dani announced.

"Oh, good grief!" Sandra sputtered as she gave a silencing wave with one heavily jeweled hand. "He's a progressive thinker, Danielle. Thanks to Clayton, Brock's Pass will be more than just a sleepy ranching community."

"Whatever," Dani responded dully. She wasn't about to enter into a debate. Besides, she was growing restless. "I think I'll go for a ride," she said, at the same moment the decision was made in her mind.

"I think that's a good idea," Sandra answered as Dani began her exit from the kitchen. "Maybe some time spent out of doors will put a bit of color in your cheeks. I swear, you're as pale and pasty as your mother was."

Dani cringed, but ignored Sandra's dig. She knew calling the older woman on it would accomplish nothing more than causing yet another fight. A nice ride in the cool morning air was far more appealing than volleying words like weapons with her aunt.

Dani was gone from the kitchen for less than ten minutes. Miraculously, Sandra was not lying in wait as she had expected. Rather, she discovered Tyler still lingering by the coffeepot.

"Are you taking the day off?" Dani asked. It came out more like a reprimand from the boss than a question.

The smile he offered was completely devoid of humor. "I thought I'd go with you. It's probably been some time since you were last on a horse."

She dismissed his suggestion immediately. "Don't be ridiculous! I've been riding since I was four years old. I certainly don't need a chaperon."

"You need a keeper," he muttered under his breath as his eyes moved over the generous curves of her body that two layers of clothing failed to completely conceal.

"What did you say?" she asked, flustered momentarily by the feel of his eyes on her.

"I said, I'm sure you're a real trouper."

"A compliment?" Dani batted her long lashes and feigned shock. Retrieving the leather gloves from her back pocket, she began pulling the first one into place. "Thanks for the offer, but I'm perfectly capable of going out on my own."

"Not up into the pass."

"What makes you think I'm going to the pass?" she asked. Even Dani had a hard time buying the innocence she had tried to inject into her question.

Tyler moved so that he stood almost on top of her. Her senses immediately tuned in to the pleasant mixture of scents filling the small gap between his body and hers. It was quite a contrast to the sensual cologne from the night before.

"Don't treat me like a fool, Danielle. You want to go looking for Jennifer. The pass is the logical place to start."

"So I'm going to ride out to the pass? So what? I'll wait for a while to meet her when she comes down off the mountain. I don't think that requires a guide."

Dani took a small step backward. She didn't like having him so close. The warmth emanating from his big body made her feel things she had no business feeling. Leaning her head back, Dani looked directly into his eyes. "You forget, Mr. Cantrell, this is my home. I'm sure I know this land far better than you."

"Don't count on it," he warned.

Brushing past him, Dani pulled on a leather coat from the peg by the back door. He stayed on her heels every step of the way.

Despite the fact that she took long, purposeful strides in an attempt to distance herself from him, he walked at her side like some sort of optimistic stray.

"I'm going alone!" she insisted between tightly clenched teeth.

"I don't think so," he countered easily as one large hand adjusted the rim of his Stetson to shield his eyes from the brilliant rays of sunshine reflecting off the mountainside.

Focusing her attention on the barn up ahead, Dani fumed silently. Why couldn't he just take her not-so-subtle hint and leave her be? The answer to her unasked question was as elusive as the reason for her mind's awareness of his every move.

Perhaps she had some little-known disease that had suddenly robbed her of the ability to think and act rationally. There were too many strange things going on. Where was Jen? Why had she taken off and left Dani in the company of a man like Tyler? And why had the dream returned? The mere fact that she was walking alongside a cowboy was reason enough to consider seeking medical attention. Add to that the fact that she couldn't seem to stop herself from noticing the fluid motion of his body, and she was a prime candidate for long-term institutionalization.

The soft sounds of a horse's contented whinny greeted her as she reached the barn door. The strong, sweet scent of hay mingled with other, less pleasant odors, but Dani didn't really notice. Moving directly to the end stall, she forgot Tyler long enough to stroke the nose of the gray mare.

"How's my girl?" Dani cooed to the horse.

The animal answered by moving forward and bowing her head for a scratch between two alert ears. Reaching into a rusted tin that was mounted on the wall, Dani produced a cube of sugar and placed it in the flat of her palm for the animal.

"Sparkle, I see you haven't lost your taste for sweets. I always liked that about you," she said softly.

A rustling at the opposite side of the barn drew her attention. Tyler collected her saddle and tack from among the collection stored against one wall. Dani momentarily wondered just how he knew which was hers.

Hoisting the heavy thing onto one shoulder, he walked over to where she stood. "You want to open the stall?" He growled his request when she remained frozen to the spot.

Dani had been silently admiring his powerful body, to the exclusion of everything else. "Of course," she said, flustered.

Tripping the latch, Dani clicked her tongue, bringing the impeccably trained animal out of the stall. Grabbing the blanket he had tossed over one shoulder, Dani laid it over the animal to keep from galling Sparkle during the ride.

"Whoa . . ." Tyler said, soothingly as he positioned the saddle at the curve of Sparkle's back.

Dani held the animal's lead while Tyler fastened and checked the placement of the creaking leather saddle. As he knelt next to the animal, his legs strained against the denim, outlining the definition of muscle beneath. Dani swallowed and schooled herself to ignore such things.

"Give me a minute to get my mount, and I'll take you up to the campsites I spotted yesterday," he said.

Nodding to him, Dani waited until he turned his back before pulling on the lead. As casually as possible, she backed the animal from the barn, while her green eyes remaining fixed on Tyler.

Once she and Sparkle were in the clear, she placed her foot in the stirrup and exerted the effort necessary to hoist her small frame into the high saddle. "Git!" she commanded, digging her booted heels into either side of the horse's underbelly.

The mare responded, and they fled the corral, hopefully leaving a cloud of dust for Tyler to inhale.

The wind freed strands of her brown hair, allowing it to whip against her face. Dani regretted that, thanks to Tyler, she'd forgotten her hat. It was just another negative to add to her ongoing mental tally.

She smiled at the feel of the air slapping her cheeks as she urged the horse in the direction of the mountain. She'd traveled a few hundred yards when her ears detected a sound that put an instant damper on her enthusiasm. One quick check over her shoulder was all the verification she required. *How had he managed to saddle a horse and catch up so damned fast?* Dani wondered.

It was pointless to try and outrun him—not when he was riding a stallion Dani knew was far faster than her Sparkle.

Easing the pressure of her knees against the animal, Dani resigned herself to his company.

"That wasn't very polite," he chided her.

"I wasn't trying to be polite," Dani responded. Her back went ramrod-straight as she glared her displeasure at him.

"I told you I was coming with you," he reminded her, as if that somehow granted him divine permission to do as he pleased.

"And I told you I didn't want company."

No more words passed between them for a long time, which was just as well. Dani needed time to get her anger in check. Losing her temper with Tyler would be nothing more than a childish waste of energy. She had no intention of giving that man a thing, not even the chewing-out he so obviously needed.

The terrain grew rough and rocky soon after they left the flat, grassy meadow at the base of the mountain. Stately evergreens stood guard on either side of the small, rutted trail, which was so narrow that they had no option but to travel single file.

Dani was astounded to discover that he did, in fact, appear to know the mountain as well as she. Tyler guided his animal through the partially hidden path with near-perfect expertise.

"Are you from around here?"

"I spent a few years around here when I was a kid."

Dani stared harder at his shoulders. "How long have you worked on the Circle B?"

"Nearly two months."

His upper body dipped and twisted in perfect rhythm to the horse's uneven gait. She struggled to keep her mind from concentrating too hard on the scene before her.

"If you've only been here two months," she began in a loud voice, "how is it you know your way around so well?"

"Great sense of direction."

"Try again," Dani said as she inched her mare closer.

Tyler glanced back at her over his shoulder before speaking. "It doesn't take a member of Mensa to know the difference between north and south."

She wrinkled her forehead and she said, "Most ranch hands haven't even heard of Mensa."

She felt the animal's hoofs beneath her slip. It reminded her of why she'd so rarely ventured onto this part of the ranch. There was always the possibility that the mare would lose her footing. Sparkle could be seriously injured—or, worse, she could fall and roll, crushing Dani with her weight.

"Look," Tyler said in a near whisper. His finger pointed to a spot between two jutting stones.

A pair of elk started at the sound of his voice. Their ears shot straight up in alarm before they bolted from the bank of the small stream.

"Nicely done," Dani offered, with a wink and a click of her tongue.

Tyler smiled at her sarcasm. A bright, brilliant smile that reached all the way to his eyes. Dani felt the intensity of his expression surge through her on a powerful flood of conflicting emotions.

So he has a great smile. So what? she told herself. *So my heart turned over at that display of even white teeth set against his ruggedly handsome face.* It was definitely time to consider consulting a mental-health professional. Perhaps when she returned to Atlanta she could get a referral from the psych department.

As promised, Tyler took her to see the remnants of campsites. They looked relatively fresh and convincing, right down to the signature way Jennifer placed stones around her fires. Always symmetrical, always in the shape of a star.

After more than three hours, Dani finally admitted to herself that she was just spinning her wheels. To Tyler, she merely said, "I think you had better be getting back."

He pulled up and turned the stallion in the opposite direction. "I'm not paid by the hour, Danielle."

There was an edge to his voice, but Dani was too distracted by her own thoughts for it to even register. "Whatever," she mumbled. Her concern for Jennifer was growing by leaps and bounds.

Scanning the thick, rocky brush, her imagination went into overdrive. There were any number of cliffs and crevasses. What if Jen's horse had fallen? Or maybe some rabid animal had attacked, leaving her weak or injured. Cupping one hand at the side of her mouth, Dani yelled, "Jenniferrrrrr!"

The words bounced and echoed through the unforgiving landscape, but produced no response. Dani tried again, with the same result.

Tyler's horse snorted and danced with apparent displeasure at the shrill female voice, then reared up on his hindquarters. Effortlessly Tyler stayed with the animal and quickly managed to quiet the spooked stallion.

"Hang in there, boy," he said as he reached and stroked the animal's neck. Lifting his head fractionally, he gave Dani a look that warned against any further screaming.

Contritely she followed him back to the barn. By the time she climbed down out of the saddle, Dani had made a decision. Handing the reins to Tyler, she muttered some excuse and moved quickly in the direction of the house.

Four hours in the saddle had left her feeling a bit stiff and sore. Ignoring the protestations from her body, she ran the entire distance to the house. When she burst into the kitchen, Dani could feel the burn of exertion on her cheeks. Her breath was coming in short, labored spurts.

Lupe stopped in mid-stir, her face melting into a series of confused wrinkles. "Are you running from the devil himself?"

"No," she said between gulps for air. "I left him brushing down the horses."

"What?"

"Never mind." Dani slipped out of the coat and replaced it on the peg near the rear door. "I need to use the car. Do you know if Aunt Sandra has any plans for the day?"

"She's gone," Lupe answered.

Dani's face fell in a frown of disappointment. "Did she say when she was coming back?"

"This afternoon sometime."

"Damn," Dani muttered.

"She's over at the Brightwoods'. Clayton is teaching her all about furniture restoration. Waste of good time, if you ask me."

"Great," she mumbled. "I'll have to use Jen's car," Dani announced, much to Lupe's obvious disapproval.

"You know she doesn't hanker much to anyone borrowing that fancy car of hers."

Dani got up on tiptoe to kiss the soft skin of the housekeeper's cheek. "She won't mind," Dani said, though she knew full well Jennifer would have a first-class fit when she found out.

After a quick bath, Dani changed into a pale skirt, gray sweater and flats. She bounded from the house with a new sense of purpose. In her hand she clutched the spare set of keys from the nightstand in her sister's bedroom.

The unattached garage was cool and smelled of stale exhaust. Carefully, Dani peeled off the tarpaulin covering the Testarossa.

"Okay, so it's nice," she said aloud as she slipped the key into the lock. "But it isn't worth the ridiculous amount of money you paid for it, Jen."

Gunning the powerful engine, Dani looked around, getting a fix on the plethora of gauges, knobs and instruments at her disposal. The thing had more options than a 747 and cost more than the average single-family home in Atlanta. Still, seated behind the polished-teak steering wheel of Jennifer's car, she felt a certain comforting closeness to her absent sister.

The trip into the town of Brock's Pass meant covering more than forty miles of oft-deserted highway. To cut the monotonous hum of the engine, Dani flipped on the radio, increasing the volume every few miles until the music blared at a deafening level.

At some point during the trip, she decided that living in Atlanta had turned her into a convenience junky. Everything she needed, wanted or desired was an easy walk from her condo. Montana was an entirely different situation—miles separated people and places, and everyone accepted the hours of commuting as a simple fact of life.

Anxiously she pulled the expensive import into a parking spot and cut the engine. A rectangular white sign with black lettering loomed above the building: Brock's Pass Sheriff's Department.

Checking her appearance in the car's rearview mirror, Dani decided she looked presentable enough, and abandoned the car after being careful to lock the doors and set the alarm.

The building smelled like coffee, cigarette smoke and citrus deodorizer. The walls of the entryway were filled with photographs depicting the succession of sheriffs since the inception of the office. Dani stopped briefly to glare at the last face in the row. Engraved on the oval brass plate beneath the heavily framed portrait was the name Bubba Cassidy. Staring at the rounded face with its pudgy cheeks, she felt a shiver of repulsion race up her spine. Bubba's smile was not only plastic, it displayed a mouthful of badly stained, crooked teeth.

She called him a vile name under her breath before moving into the large, open office space.

A young woman dressed in a tight but official-looking uniform peered up from her seat at a typewriter. "Can I help you?"

"I'd like to see Sheriff Cassidy," Dani replied.

"Not here," the girl said, before blowing a large pink bubble that eventually burst and stuck to her lower lip.

Dani sighed and refrained from lecturing the girl on office etiquette. "Do you know when he'll be back?"

She shrugged her shoulders, and Dani found herself amazed by the fact that her shirt button held. The fabric was so tight against the girl's generous bosom that Dani actually toyed with the idea of finding a way to make her sneeze, just to see what might happen.

"He's over to the luncheonette," she said, the gum popping with each syllable.

"Thanks."

Deciding the car was safest in the parking lot of the only law enforcement agency around, Dani set out for the restaurant on foot.

Mary's Luncheonette was something of a landmark in Brock's Pass, with its Formica counters, turquoise vinyl stools and fresh, though less than memorable, food. Mary herself had died near the end of World War II, leaving the operation in the capable hands of her many children.

In order to reach Mary's, Dani had to walk the six or seven blocks that basically encompassed the town in its entirety. Many buildings retained their original wood exteriors, which made the newer, brick structures stand out like invasive bacteria beneath a microscope.

Looking ahead, Dani spotted a new sign indicating that an architect had set up shop in the space next to Quigley's. Quigley's was the local equivalent of a convenience store. While there was a wide variety of foodstuffs and staples on the shelves, they charged top dollar for each and every item.

Dani glanced through the window of the overpriced grocery store, half expecting to see a familiar face. She stopped dead in her tracks when she spied Tyler in line at the checkout, his arms cradling two bottles of grape juice and a box of tea bags. Alarms went off. Stepping to the side, Dani shielded herself in the afternoon shadows, her eyes fixed on the deceitful creep inside the store.

She asked herself if there could be a logical explanation for Tyler purchasing those particular items. The refrigerator back at the ranch was full of those supplies. "So why is he buying more?" she asked aloud.

"Danielle Baylor!"

She jumped at the enthusiastic voice. "Carol!" she exclaimed upon turning. The joy of seeing her old friend and confidante made her momentarily forget her prey.

"You look wonderful," the tall redhead gushed.

"So do you!" Dani returned, with genuine admiration and just a twinge of the old envy. Carol Marshall had one of those willowy figures that made her look like a model no matter what she wore. The years had been more than kind, for Carol's pretty features had only heightened in ten years.

"Nuts!" Dani moaned when she glanced over her shoulder and found that Tyler had vanished. "Carol, I'm sorry but I've got to run. Call me out at the ranch, and we'll get together and catch up."

"Count on it!" Carol yelled as Dani ran into the store.

"Do you know Tyler Cantrell—the tall man that was here just a second ago?" Dani hurriedly asked the cashier.

The girl swooned at the mere mention of the name. "You bet!"

"Where did he go?"

The girl pointed toward the rear of the store in the vicinity of an orange Exit sign. "Out the back way."

"Great," Dani groaned as she maneuvered herself sideways down an aisle blocked by a shopping cart.

The door opened onto a parking lot that contained a number of crushed beer cans and crumpled cigarette packs—but no Tyler.

With her shoulders slumped forward in defeat, Dani made her way back to the front of the store. Ignoring the curious stare of the libidinous cashier, she took a bit of her frustration out on the door by smacking it open.

Her failure to keep Tyler in her sights did little to improve her mood. By the time she reached the luncheonette, a dark scowl distorted her pretty features.

The smell of smoke, grease and coffee permeated the place. But it was the noise she noticed, above all else. The incessant clanging of pots punctuated the boisterous sounds of laughter, which was male-sounding and from the gut, and the kind that was usually the result of some off-color remark. Following one particularly unpleasant sound, her eyes fell on the man who was the object of her search.

The sight of Sheriff Cassidy was enough to bring on a rush of abhorrent emotions recalling that night so long ago. "You aren't seventeen anymore," she whispered to herself between nervously clenched teeth.

Approaching the table on a cloud of apprehension, Dani recognized the three men seated there. The youngest occupant was Don Triggs, who was either the mayor or some sort of state legislator when he wasn't hawking insurance. Justin Merriweather was there, too. He now looked to be about three years older than dirt. Dani's eyes targeted a fat, bald man dressed from head to toe in khaki, a large wad of chewing tobacco in his cheek.

With her shoulders squared, Dani walked right up to the edge of the table. An immediate and deafening silence was her initial greeting.

"Sheriff Cassidy, I'd like a moment of your time."

He rolled toward one side and retrieved a spittoon from beneath the chair and spit. Dani felt her stomach turn at the clanging sound of the liquid meeting the brass container.

"Don, old boy, scoot yourself on over and give the little lady room to sit herself down." The man complied with the sheriff's wishes, but Dani remained standing.

"This is a private matter," Dani informed him politely, though with enough firmness to get his attention away from the front of her sweater.

"In that case—" he hoisted his rotund body along the bench and slithered out of the booth "—let's you and me head on back to my office." Grunting from the effort, Sheriff Cassidy bent and retrieved his hat from the seat and placed it on his head. "Don't I know you?" he asked suddenly.

"Yes, I'm Danielle Baylor."

She could all but hear the gears of his small brain cranking through the past until a light dawned in his dull blue eyes. "Milt Baylor's youngest," he announced proudly.

"Yes."

"I thought you was back east somewheres," he said, conversationally, as they made their exit.

"I live in Atlanta," she supplied, trying not to cringe when he placed a stubby hand at the center of her back to guide her out the door.

"Never been there," he said. "'Course, I've never had a hankering to go noplace 'cept here."

It shows, she thought, but instead responded with a tight smile.

"Seems I recall something about you and Sam—"

Dani interrupted him impatiently. "Sheriff, I'm here about my sister, Jennifer."

"The vet?"

"Yes," she answered, struggling to keep her patience. "She went up into the mountains six days ago, and no one's seen her since."

Scraping his hand against his chin, the sheriff appeared to be digesting the information before he leaned near the curb and spit, yet again. "Doc Baylor's kinda got a reputation for hanging out in the woods."

Answering in a rapid succession of words, Dani could only hope that if she gave him enough details, he'd at least look into it. "Jennifer is fond of camping. Normally I wouldn't give this a second thought. But she failed to meet my plane yesterday, and that isn't at *all* like my sister."

Dani was forced to walk beside him in a silence that was broken only by the occasional sound of his spittle contacting the concrete walk. When they reached the headquarters, she carefully avoided his hand by choosing to follow him inside.

"You turned your pager off again," the gum-popping, typist/officer chided when she peered up from her desk.

Guiltily, Sheriff Cassidy reached down and fiddled with the small black instrument strapped to his belt. "Sorry about that, Bambi."

Bambi? Dani's brain screamed.

"I've been trying to reach you for the past five minutes or so," Bambi said. Her head bobbed from side to side with each new word. "Mack Grayson called in a fire over off highway 7."

Dani cut in. "Where off highway 7?"

"Just this side of the Circle B," Bambi bubbled.

Dani felt a wave of relief wash over her, mingled with a sense of regret. While she was glad to know it had nothing to do with the ranch, it was obvious that the sheriff was going out to the fire.

"If you haven't heard from your sister by the end of the week, give Bambi here a call and we'll figure something out."

Dani nodded in defeat. She wasn't convinced Bambi could help her find Jennifer. In fact, she doubted Bambi could figure out the correct time of day without some assistance.

The sheriff raced out of the building with Dani closely following. He peeled out of the parking lot before she even had an opportunity to disarm and unlock the car door.

Maybe it was just as well that Dani hadn't officially involved the sheriff. Lord knew, Aunt Sandra wouldn't have liked it. And, she reminded herself, she was probably worrying over nothing.

Just as she had during the drive from the airport, Dani optimistically looked forward to the possibility that Jennifer would be waiting for her back at the house.

Her mind drifted back to her walk through town, and again she wondered about Tyler. Why had he been in Quigley's buying the ingredients for Jennifer's favorite drink? "And why did he sneak out the back door?"

Maybe he didn't, her logical mind argued. Perhaps he had parked behind the building and had innocently made his exit via the most convenient means.

Dani's foot moved to the brake pedal as she neared a funnel of smoke towering into the sky where flames danced high into the air. She was third in the line of traffic stopped by the placement of the water truck in the center of the road. Even with the windows tightly closed, the acrid smell of the fire permeated the interior of the car.

Ignoring the black soot raining down, Dani turned off the engine, exited the car, and stood up on the running board. A huge rectangle burned out of control, oblivious of the three hoses of high-pressure water arching into it. The smell was so bad that she tugged the neck of her sweater up over her nose in an attempt to filter out the stench.

She watched for over an hour as the fire fighters battled the blaze into submission. Dani, along with the rest of the roadside voyeurs, was trapped due to the position of the tank truck. There simply was nothing to do but lean against the car and patiently wait for the firemen to finish their job. Still, if Aunt Sandra was planning a party, she was bound to catch hell for coming back so late from her wasted jaunt into town. Not to mention Jennifer's reaction to the layer of dark soot that was beginning to cover the import.

"Thank you," Dani mumbled sarcastically when it appeared the road was about to be cleared.

When the car in front of her inched forward, Dani sat frozen, her eyes fixed on the name written in bold black script across the mailbox in front of the burned trailer. "Cantrell," she read aloud.

A horn blasted, forcing Dani to turn the car onto the shoulder.

Sheriff Cassidy stood a few yards away, making notations as he talked to one of the sooty-faced firemen. Dani wasted no time before going up to him.

"Whose place is this?" she asked without preamble.

The men exchanged confused looks before Sheriff Cassidy spoke. "I thought you'd know. Why, this here's Tyler Cantrell's house."

The whine of a siren grew louder on approach. A black station wagon bearing the name of the only funeral home in Brock's Pass pulled in just behind its police escort.

Could Tyler be in there? she asked herself.

"Was someone in there?" Dani demanded, grabbing a handful of the fat officer's shirt.

"Afraid so," he answered glibly, and reached up to remove her hand. "I think you'd best run along now, Miss Baylor. I'll be in touch if we need any additional information from you."

Dani felt drained as she numbly walked back to the car and headed for the ranch. She felt an overwhelming sense of guilt for all the rotten thoughts she'd had about the man during the past twenty-four hours. It was eerie and disarming.

But not as eerie as pulling into the drive, only to find Tyler waiting for her on the porch.

Chapter Three

Dani barely managed to throw the car in Park before leaping out and making a mad dash for where Tyler stood casually chatting with her uncle.

"Didn't you see it?" she shouted as she pointed toward the west.

"See what?" Matt asked, his whitish eyebrows drawn together.

"The fire!"

"What fire?" Tyler demanded.

"Your trailer!"

All expression drained from the tall man's face. "What about my place?" He grabbed her upper arms, his fingers digging painfully into the tender flesh beneath. When she paused just long enough to catch a much-needed breath, Tyler gave her a gentle shake. "What about my place?" he repeated.

"The whole thing went up in flames," she explained. "The sheriff said something about a body—"

Dani never had an opportunity to finish the sentence, because Tyler grabbed the keys from her hand

and took off like a man possessed. The scent of burning rubber filled the air as he peeled off behind the wheel of Jennifer's car.

"Good heavens," Matt muttered. "It was just a trailer. Most of his stuff's here, so he couldn't have lost much more than some bits of furniture."

"Uncle Matt!" Dani wailed. "Didn't you hear me? There was a body in the trailer."

Matt scratched his head, apparently confused. "Cassidy must have been mistaken. No one was living in the trailer just now. The generator blew. That's why Ty's been staying with us."

"They called Singletary's," Dani argued, though she found it comfortingly easy to accept the notion that the sheriff had made a mistake. Mentally she added that it wouldn't be the first time, either.

"They call the undertaker every time they come across a dead critter in the road," Matt snorted. "Give's them something to do between funerals."

"That's disgusting," Dani said, though the twinkle of laughter in her eyes belied the protest.

Gripping her uncle's arm, Dani steered him toward the house. "Has there been any word from Jennifer?"

"Nope."

"Aunt Sandra thinks she'll show up in time for tonight's dinner with the Brightwoods."

"I'm sure she will," Matt agreed as he patted the top of her hand. "Your sister enjoys sparring with old Clayton."

Dani's grin broadened at the thought of her opinionated sister and Clayton Brightwood seated at the same table. She wouldn't be at all surprised if World War III were to result from such a scenario.

"It's about time you showed up!"

The sound of her aunt's shrill reprimand erased the smile from Dani's face.

"The Brightwoods will be here in less than an hour," she explained as her eyes roamed disapprovingly over Dani's appearance. "Do go up and make yourself presentable. I won't have you sitting down for dinner looking like some starving coed. And what *is* that awful smell?"

Lifting the sleeve of her sweater to her nose, Dani had to admit the odor was an unpleasant one. "I had to wait for a fire on highway 7."

"Well, it smells god-awful! Make certain you put that rag where it won't reek up the whole house."

Sandra went back to the list in front of her on the table. Dani knew she'd been effectively dismissed. Matt quietly dropped her hand and went in the direction of the library, probably in search of a few fingers of the bourbon that was stashed between two volumes of Shakespeare.

While Dani would have enjoyed a long soak and an early night, she knew full well that her aunt would interpret such behavior as the height of selfishness. The usual punishment for ignoring an Aunt Sandra edict was several days of silence, followed by several more days of the woman glaring her hatred.

Accepting her fate, Dani slipped out of her sweater and skirt and placed them on hangers. It was with just a touch of mean-spiritedness that she left the odoriferous clothing dangling in the doorway of her bedroom.

After washing and drying her hair, she carefully twisted the light chestnut-colored strands into a neat French braid. Examining her reflection, she decided the style gave her an air of aloofness she assumed would be lost on Sam Brightwood.

Purposefully Dani selected a simple white blouse with a high, lacy neckline to go with her black slacks. The ensemble was bland and boring, and the only visible splash of color was the devilish glint in her green eyes. There was no possible way she'd be accused of "coming on" to Sam Brightwood, not when she looked ridiculously like a steak-house waitress.

Even though nearly a decade had passed, Dani still found spending any time with the Brightwoods a distasteful task. After one final look in the mirror, she checked her watch and went scurrying for the stairs. Aunt Sandra hated what she deemed "theatrical" entrances—unless they were hers. Then the rules changed.

The house smelled of freshly baked rolls and garlic. Dani's mouth began to water even before she joined her aunt and uncle in the formal dining room. Aunt Sandra stood next to the server, fiddling with a platter of puff-pastry appetizers nestled on a crisp white doily. One perfectly drawn-on eyebrow rose questioningly as the older woman gave Dani a decidedly unflattering once-over.

"Really?" Sandra groaned through her ruby red lips. "Surely you have *something* in your closet more flattering than . . . that."

Feigning innocence, Dani smoothed the lace at her throat. "I'm sorry you don't like my outfit," she returned and walked over to the bar next to her uncle.

"I think you look just fine," Matt whispered close to her ear.

She poured herself a glass of soda just as the grandfather clock in the hallway chimed the hour. "What time are you expecting the Brightwoods?" Dani asked.

"Any moment," Sandra answered as she smoothed the folds of her dress. It was patterned with bold neon patches far too young for a woman of Sandra's years or inches. "Clayton and Sam are normally quite punctual."

"Maybe they fell into the same black hole as Jennifer," Dani suggested.

Sandra shot her a warning look. "I'm sure your sister will show up in her own good time. Just as I'm sure she'll have a reasonable explanation for her behavior. Now, let it drop, Danielle. I don't plan on having you spend the evening whining about Jennifer not meeting your plane. No one likes to listen to you whine, least of all me."

"Yes, Aunt Sandra," Dani said with a sigh.

Turning to her uncle, she noticed a distracted look in his eyes. His face was drawn into a pensive frown. "Is something wrong?"

Matt's head snapped up, the motion effectively erasing the expression that had inspired her question. "No, not a thing," he answered, forcing a note of cheerfulness into his voice.

The sound of the doorbell signaled the arrival of the Brightwoods. Dani felt her skin crawl at the thought, but plastered a smile on her face in deference to Sandra and in an attempt to prevent giving her aunt any more fuel for the fire of her vengeance. She owed the woman something for acting as a stand-in after her parents' death. *Surely whatever debt I owe her must be paid by now—with interest!* Dani added silently.

Clayton Brightwood ambled into the living room with all the grace and finesse of the cattle he raised. Dani was surprised to find that the long, straight hair slicked back on his head was still black as pitch, even though he was well into his sixties. His face was somewhat crinkled from age, though his dark eyes appeared to have retained their youthful clarity. The jacket he'd chosen to complement his white shirt with its silver tipped collar was tan, which seemed to magnify his height and circumference. The sound of his bootheels hitting the polished wood floor echoed loudly.

"Danielle, nice to see you again," Clayton said as he reached out for her hand.

"Mr. Brightwood," she said politely as he bowed his head to place a damp kiss near her third knuckle.

Looking past him, Dani caught her first sight of Sam Brightwood in several years. She was amazed by what she saw. Just as tall as his father, but far more handsome, Sam had dark hair and eyes the color of a gray winter morning.

Reluctantly Sam shuffled across the floor in her direction, his head slightly bowed in what appeared to be a genuine display of remorse. Was it possible? Was he finally willing to admit that he had been the one at fault?

"Hi, Dani," he said in a soft voice, but made no move to touch her.

"Sam."

"You look—"

Sam was silenced by the boom of the front door crashing open.

Tyler rushed into the room, trailed by a waddling Sheriff Cassidy. Every face in the room froze in mid-expression at the sudden and unexpected intrusion.

"What is going on here?" Sandra demanded.

Tyler walked directly toward Dani, easing his broad shoulders between the two Brightwood men so that he stood towering in front of her. She looked into his eyes and felt herself tense at what she saw there. Pain, raw and deep, emanated from the dark pools.

"Dani, I'm afraid I have some terrible news for you."

"Jennifer." She choked out the word, her hands going to her throat.

Tyler nodded. "I'm sorry, Dani. Jennifer was in the trailer. She's dead."

His face disintegrated into a series of disconnected dots before fading completely to black.

IN THE WEEKS following Jennifer's death, spring had turned to summer, filling the air with the sweet scent of wildflowers. He watched her from the shadows of the barn. The trip back to Atlanta had done her some good. Hopefully, it had allowed her to get some per-spective on the situation. Not to mention the added benefit of putting several hundred miles between Dani and her aunt Sandra.

During her absence, Tyler had paid close attention to Sandra. The woman seemed to have a strong dislike for her niece. Lifting his hat from his head, he wiped the band of perspiration with the back of his hand and tossed aside his tools.

He moved slowly, careful not to make a sound as he sneaked up behind her.

"It's a start," she said to the horses grazing just the other side of the fence.

"What's a start?"

Dani turned, and her expression registered surprise at seeing him. He wondered if she was coping. At least she no longer cried uncontrollably, he decided. But there was a definite sadness in her big green eyes. A sadness that made him want to pull her to him.

"What's it to you?" she returned. She offered him her back and pretended to concentrate on the horses, the flowers, the cloudless sky—anything but him.

The knowledge filled him with a definite feeling of arrogant manliness. The pleasant scent of her perfume was carried to him on the gentle breeze. He doubted whether the heat surging in his body was because of the strong afternoon sun.

"Actually," he began as he moved beside her and placed one expensive boot on the lowest rail of the fence, "it's nothing to me. I just thought you might want someone less hostile than Sandra to talk to."

Dani turned her head, tilted it back and studied the expression on his face. He made sure there was none.

"I don't think you're less hostile, Mr. Cantrell. You're just hostile in a different way."

"You think I'm hostile? Is that why you stay in your room until I leave in the morning and make certain our contact is kept to a minimum?"

"I just don't like you," Dani answered with a superior smile.

Tyler tilted back the brim of his Stetson, genuinely surprised by her answer. "What is it you don't like?"

Dani let out a breath of apparent frustration. "Does it make a difference? Can't you just accept the fact that I find you annoying, and leave it at that?"

"It makes a difference," he said, in a voice so soft that it could barely be heard through the collection of muffled outdoor sounds.

"Look," she said. He saw her entire body tense. "Uncle Matt says the new trailer will be here in a week or so. After that, you and I will not have to have any contact. Consequently, what I think of you, and why, is irrelevant."

"Do you always speak to people in that snotty tone, or is it just for my benefit?"

He noticed her hands were clenched tightly into fists. "Go away."

He couldn't stop the smile that he knew began as a twinkle in his eyes. It traveled down to turn up the corners of his mouth. "I'll go away as soon as you tell me what it is about me that you don't like."

"Fine, but remember, *you* asked for this."

Squaring her shoulders, Dani obviously was miffed by the fact that his height forced her to crane her neck in order to meet his eyes.

"I don't like cowboys in general. I don't like you, specifically, because you have this air about you that simply grates on my nerves. I don't like the fact that you seem to have taken over the main house as if you were lord of the manor. I don't like, nor do I understand, why you wear boots that cost more than two months' pay."

"So it's my boots you don't like."

"Don't trivialize my opinions!"

"You're the one condemning me because of my footwear."

It looked as if she had to struggle to suppress her urge to scream. "Right," she said with a huff. "Think what you want."

She turned to retreat. Tyler reached out and gripped the smooth skin of her upper arm. "We haven't finished our little talk here," he said.

"You may not be finished," she said as she tried to shake free. "I'm finished. So let go."

"We need to talk," he said. Tyler managed to keep his voice calm and even.

"We do not *need* to talk, Mr. Cantrell."

Tossing his head back, Tyler laughed at her.

"Let go of my arm!"

"If I let go of your arm, will you stay here?"

"No."

"Then you have left me no option but to detain you until we have an opportunity to finish our little chat."

Dani must have hoped the narrowing of her eyes conveyed her fury. "Say whatever it is you want to say."

"Was that a compromise?" he asked, prodding. He knew he shouldn't be enjoying this verbal sparring, he just couldn't help it.

He found the touch of anger shining in her eyes appealing. Just as he admired the way she seemed determined to keep him in his place. What, he wondered, would she think of him when she discovered the truth? Then and there, Tyler knew he wanted to delay that happening. The trick would be in creating a diversion that would give him time.

"It's not a compromise," she assured him with a shake of her head. "The sooner you talk, the sooner you'll let me go back up to the house."

"Have you always been this stubborn and opinionated?"

"Get on with it, Cantrell." Dani turned her head slightly and fixed her eyes on a pebble near her right foot.

"I didn't tell the sheriff or you the whole truth about Jennifer's death."

At that, Dani's head snapped up, and her eyes met his.

Taking a deep breath and clearing his throat, Tyler continued, "Jennifer didn't happen to wander into my trailer that day."

Dani shook her head as if clearing away a fog. "Very gallant of you to keep your relationship with my sister a secret."

"You don't understand," he said as he shuffled his weight from foot to foot, like a child admitting to a lie. "Jennifer and I weren't involved. She hired me."

"I know that," Dani returned.

It was evident from her stiff posture that she was feeling frustrated by her continued captivity.

"Uncle Matt told me that Jen had been the one to hire—"

"Listen!" he barked, giving her a start.

"I'm listening. Okay?"

"Jennifer didn't hire me as just a foreman." Reaching behind him, Tyler produced a small leather case and flipped it open with a flick of his wrist.

"Licensed private detective?" Dani read. "State of Maryland?"

"Jennifer wanted me to look into your parents' murder."

"Wait a minute. Are you telling me that all that time I was worried sick about my sister, you knew she was safely tucked away at the trailer?"

Tyler's grip on her arm tightened fractionally. He was suddenly very afraid that she might turn tail and run. He thought and spoke quickly.

"Neither Jennifer nor I believed that the case was properly investigated. She wanted me to look into it without attracting any attention."

"If the case was so poorly investigated, why did Stone commit suicide after he was found guilty?"

"I don't know."

"I think that was pretty damning behavior."

"Maybe it was," Tyler said.

For several seconds he watched the expressions warring in her eyes. It wasn't until he was relatively sure that she would stay with him that Tyler allowed his hand to fall away.

"Your sister tracked me down and devised this scheme to bring you back here."

"Are you trying to tell me that Jennifer was in your trailer the entire time I was sitting at home worried?"

Tyler nodded.

"Jennifer would never have done something like that to me."

"She agonized over it for a long time," Tyler supplied. "She needed you back here so that the nightmare would come back."

Dani reached up and ran her fingers through her hair. "I just don't believe this. And why didn't you tell me? You could have said something when we were alone. If you'd have stopped glaring at me for one second, you could have explained this elaborate plan to me, and then taken me to see Jen."

"I didn't mean to glare," he said softly. "Jennifer warned me that if I so much as threw one drop of charm your way, you'd run like hell."

"So the arrogance, the insulting looks, all of that was just scripted behavior to keep me in the dark?"

"I'm telling you the truth, Dani," he said.

Tyler reached out for her and pulled her gently against his chest. It felt good to hold her, he decided. It felt good to have his hands gently patting her back.

He felt her grab handfuls of his shirt, and he heard her suck in a deep breath. Then his chest exploded when he felt her small body begin to convulse with sobs. He looked up, wondering how everything had gotten so complicated. If only he'd met her on different terms. If only he were someone else.

As her crying subsided, Dani felt a myriad of new sensations replacing her grief. She was too aware of the corded muscles of his chest. Too aware of the powerful thighs pressed against her. Too aware of the feel of his heartbeat against her cheek. Realizing the direction of her thoughts, she pushed away from him, dabbing at her eyes with the backs of her hands.

"Why would Jen concoct this after all these years? She knew the nightmare was nothing more than the flawed memory of a six-year-old child," Dani countered. "It doesn't make sense that she would need me here in Montana to rehash old news."

"Then why was she murdered?"

"Excuse me?" Dani felt her jaw drop in utter disbelief.

"The pattern of the fire could be consistent with the use of an accelerant."

"I suppose now you're going to tell me that you're some sort of expert on fires?"

"I used to be an arson investigator for an insurance company in Baltimore."

Throwing her hands in the air, Dani allowed them to slap the sides of her jeans. "This gets better and better. A hired foreman is standing on my ranch telling me that my sister was murdered, even though it's been ruled an accident by the authorities."

"Those same authorities didn't believe you when you filed your complaint against Sam, either. Bubba Cassidy is about as incompetent as a person can get."

"Where are you getting all your information?" Dani asked as she met his eyes.

"Jennifer. And some discreet inquiries of my own."

"This is crazy," Dani said, blinking her eyes in the hope that this was all a dream—a bad dream that would be forgotten shortly after awakening.

"What if Jennifer was right?" Tyler implored as his hands reached out and captured her just above the elbows. "What if she and I were getting too close to the truth about your parents' murders? It would explain a lot about the fire."

"If she wanted my help, why didn't she just call me in Atlanta?"

"She knew you only had the dreams here. She also knew she would need your support on a full investigation."

"What does that mean?"

"Jennifer wanted to tell you about the inconsistencies we'd uncovered while you were here. She told me that she wanted to make certain she had your okay to continue probing."

Letting out a breath, Dani took in the pained expression on his face. "You're telling me the truth, aren't you?" It wasn't really a question, and he didn't respond. "What happens now? Do we call Cassidy and tell him that the trailer fire wasn't accidental?"

Tyler shook his head. "Cassidy isn't good for much more than spitting on the sidewalk. Besides, he was in an incredible hurry to have the fire ruled accidental. He vetoed the fire chief's suggestion that they get some help from the state boys."

"So we just let whoever did this get away with it?"

"Not by a long shot," Tyler answered, with reassuring conviction in his tone. "We have to do this carefully. Obviously Jennifer and I weren't careful enough.''

''What was she doing at the time she was . . . ?''

''I don't know,'' Tyler said as he slapped his hat against his pant leg. ''She told me that she was going to hang out at the trailer, going over the transcript from the trial. The last time I saw her was about an hour and a half before you came home and told me about the fire.''

''I assume she was fine then.''

''You got it,'' he said as he adjusted his hat. ''I told her I thought I had seen you in town, and so we decided to meet later in the evening. Jennifer said she thought she had found something significant in the transcript.''

''What was it?''

''She didn't have time to say. She promised to outline it for me when we got together later that night.''

''So we need to get another copy of the transcript, right?''

''Wait a second!'' Tyler said skeptically. ''Is this the same 'Sorry, but I don't like you' Danielle?''

''Don't push me, Cantrell,'' she warned him. ''I need you.''

''I'm flattered.''

''Not like that,'' she said as she slapped in the vicinity of his chest. ''I need you to help me find out if my sister was murdered.''

''I think we need to be very careful about investigating this. I don't want whoever's behind this to think you've picked up where Jennifer left off.''

Dani thought for a second and then suggested, "How about letting people think we're dating?"

She looked up at his boyish grin and the anticipation in his eyes and found herself smiling from embarrassment. "Pretending, Cantrell. We can start by going to dinner tonight."

"I'd like that. I'm *really* flattered," he said with a wink.

"Don't be. I'm only using you to escape Aunt Sandra for an evening." Dani turned and began to walk back toward the house. She refused to acknowledge the lightness in her step, or attribute the fluttering in her stomach to Tyler.

"Be ready by six," she heard him call, but only waved her hand as a signal that she had heard him.

"Why are you grinning?"

"No real reason," Dani answered her aunt, who was making a profession out of mourning Jennifer. Dani instantly thought of her sister's death being intentional and felt the smile fade from her face.

"Show some respect, would you, Danielle?"

"Yes, Aunt Sandra."

Dani backed out of the kitchen, wondering if her aunt could have had a hand in Jennifer's death. "Tyler's made me paranoid!"

"What's Ty done now?"

"Nothing," she said, answering her uncle. "I didn't see you" she said as she got on tiptoe to place a kiss on his cheek.

"Are you okay?" Matt's voice echoed the concern she noted in his expression.

"Of course," she assured him.

"Dani, I couldn't bear it if something . . ."

She placed her finger to his lips. "I'm fine, really. I'm going to take a long bath, and then Tyler and I are going into town this evening."

"Let me get this straight." Matt scratched his head. "You and Tyler have plans to do something together?"

"Yes. Is that some sort of crime?"

"No, but the two of you haven't exactly taken to one another."

"For goodness' sake, Uncle Matt. We're going to dinner and a movie, not registering for a silver pattern."

"Sorry," he said as he placed a hand on her cheek. "I'm glad, really. I think it's good for you to have a friend."

When she heard the clock chime, Dani kissed her uncle's cheek and bolted for the stairs. "I've got to get moving. Be sweet and tell Aunt Sandra I won't be here for dinner, would you?"

"Throwing me into the fire, huh?"

"I heard that, Matthew!" Dani and Matt exchanged conspiratorial smiles as the sound of Sandra's cackle echoed through the house.

DANI WENT THROUGH her closet twice before settling on a pair of jeans and a green silk blouse for the evening. Sucking in her breath in an attempt to calm her nerves and erase the shake from her hand, she finally managed to put the matching green bow in her hair where her French braid ended. "Be calm, this isn't a *real* date. Tyler and I are just doing this so that we can find the truth about Jen's death." Her reflection belied her statements. "I don't even remember my last date!" she told herself. After a brief discussion with her image in the mirror, she finally found the courage to go downstairs.

Instead of finding Tyler in the living room, as she had expected, she encountered Aunt Sandra at the foot of the stairs, lying in wait.

"What a shame you went to all that trouble for nothing," Sandra said, in the sarcastically sweet tone that had haunted Dani throughout her childhood.

"All what trouble?" Dani countered.

"He left."

"Who left?"

"Tyler," her aunt supplied, with undisguised malice in her tone.

"Is that so?" Dani asked, noting that Sandra's evil expression hinted that there was more to come. Bracing her body against the wall, she waited for her aunt to drop the next little bomb.

"He received a call while you were busy draining the hot-water heater for your bath. It was very selfish of you to use all the water, but so typical of your behavior."

"Is there a point here?" Dani asked.

"Of course there's a point. Buck just left to take Tyler to the airport."

"Thank you for passing that information along," Dani said. "I'll give Carol a call and see if she's free for the evening."

"Don't you want to know who called him?"

Dani tried not to choke on her aunt's heavy perfume as she attempted to pass where the woman stood guard at the base of the stairs.

"It's none of my business," Dani responded.

"I just thought you'd like to know why he was standing you up."

"I don't want to know."

Sandra countered Dani's move, preventing her from escaping the trap the older woman had set at the bottom of the stairs. "A woman called, and he went running without so much as a look back in your direction."

Chapter Four

"I even called Baltimore!" Dani grumbled into her third mug of beer. "He showed me his private detective's license from there."

"Did you learn anything significant?" Carol asked.

Shrugging, Dani tipped slightly in the high-backed kitchen chair. "I learned native Baltimorians are incapable of formulating a sentence that doesn't include the word *hon*."

"I guess that isn't helpful."

"Brilliant deduction, Carol."

"Hey, Dani—" her friend's voice was slurred "—if I wanted abuse, I would have gone along with Greg and the kids."

"Sorry," she said, meeting the other woman's pale blue eyes. "Speaking of which, I hope you didn't stay home on my account."

The redhead tossed her head back. Dani noted that her laughter came from deep within her. "You gave me the perfect excuse to stay home."

"We don't like our in-laws?"

"About as much as you like Slithering Sandra."

Then it was Dani's turn to laugh. "I had forgotten that nickname."

"It'll stay with me forever," Carol said as she got up to fill their glasses for a fourth time. "She was so hateful to you when we were growing up. If you would have ended up a serial killer, I was all set to appear on 'Oprah' to explain your awful treatment at the hands of your sadistic aunt."

Shrugging, she accepted a full mug from Carol and lifted it to her mouth, enjoying the bitter coldness as it slid down her throat. "I wonder whether Tyler will come back," she said. Then, after seeing her companion's reaction, she wished she had kept her thoughts to herself.

"Are you getting involved with that guy?" Carol asked, in the cautionary tone Dani had heard her use on her three children.

"Not really," Dani answered after reviewing their short-lived truce in her head.

" 'Not really, I wish we were,' or 'Not really, I hope the guy crashes and burns on his return flight'?"

Suddenly antsy, Dani rose and paced unsteadily on the kitchen tiles. "Have you ever instinctively known that something was bad for you, yet you still felt compelled to seek it out?"

"Anything chocolate," Carol answered.

Dani smiled. "I was going for something a bit more important."

"No, I think you are going for Tyler," Carol said, a serious light shining in her eyes.

"Crazy, huh?" Dani asked as she returned to her seat.

"A little beyond crazy. He's a nice enough guy," Carol began. "It's just the fact that no one seems to know anything about him. He seems to have simply appeared here one day, and he stays pretty much to himself."

"I'm acting crazy, huh?"

Carol nodded.

"I don't know why I'm so intrigued by him. It's not rational."

"It doesn't have to be rational, Dani," Carol explained. "Maybe I'm just suggesting that you take things slowly where Tyler is concerned. I think you need to know something about him. Something that would explain why your sister hired him, when he isn't exactly a cowboy by trade."

"You're right," Dani sighed. "I'm acting like a fool who has just discovered the opposite sex." She took another sip from her glass.

"He is gorgeous though...." Carol sighed wistfully. "He's the kind of guy my mother told me she would send me to a convent if I so much as thought about dating."

"Let's change the subject," Dani insisted. The words seemed slurred, even to her alcohol-soaked brain. "Obviously I'll have to call Uncle Matt for a ride home. I can't believe a few beers has me teetering on the edge of drunkenness."

"As long as you don't drive, what's the harm in an occasional tipping of the glass?"

"Nothing, I suppose. It's how Uncle Matt spends most of his evenings."

"Can you blame him? If I lived with your aunt, I'd probably be driven to drink, as well."

"Let me call Uncle Matt," she said, rising to move in the direction of the wall phone. "Shoot!" she said, looking down to see what had caused the dull pain in the arch of her bared foot. A small blue building block had attached itself. As she peeled the little bugger off, she noted that four circles had been tattooed on her skin.

"Sorry," Carol grumbled. "My kids won't win any awards for neatness."

"No problem," Dani lied. Lifting the receiver, she hugged it to her chest and looked at her friend. "Remember when we were kids, how we spent hours in the summertime pulling prank calls on Sandra?"

"That was fun," Carol agreed with a wistful smile. "Caller ID has crippled all future generations."

"I never thought of that," Dani said as she placed her finger on the wall unit to silence the chastising voice that was telling her to either make a call or hang up. "Let's hope Uncle Matt gets the phone."

Carol crossed the fingers of both her hands. The action was slightly dulled by the quantity of alcohol she had consumed.

Dani had to concentrate hard on the keypad to dial her home. On the third ring, her uncle said, "Hello."

"Hi, it's me. Can you send someone to get me at Carol's? I've had a little too much to drink."

"You?" The male voice rose an octave in apparent disbelief.

"Please, Uncle Matt?" Dani asked. "And *please* don't tell Sandra that I went visiting and got pasted. She'll harp for weeks."

"I'll organize your rescue, honey. Don't give it a thought."

"Thanks," she whispered before replacing the receiver on its hook.

"Matt running interference?"

"Yes," she said as she returned to her seat. "I don't know what I would do without Matt," she mused, pushing the half-empty mug away toward the center of the round oak table.

"You always have been his favorite.... I mean... I'm sorry Dani," Carol murmured. "I wasn't thinking."

"I've adjusted," Dani insisted. "I miss Jennifer more than I can say, but I've put her death into perspective." *It's the possibility that she was murdered that keeps me from sleeping nights.*

"Still, I shouldn't have said something so callous."

"It's no problem," Dani insisted.

Nearly an hour of chitchat passed before the doorbell sounded and she rose, giving her friend a tight squeeze. "That must be someone from the Circle B."

"Think we can make it to the door without falling on our faces?" Carol asked.

"Not a problem," Dani said. "Okay," she said after swaying slightly as she stood up, "small problem."

"Not for me," Carol stated emphatically. "I can just go into my room and crash until the terrible trio returns from their visit with the wicked witch."

"Is your mother-in-law really that terrible?" Dani asked as they started down the hallway toward the door.

"Death would become her," Carol answered without the slightest hesitation as she pulled open the door. "Well, thank God my mother isn't around to see this."

"Excuse me?" Tyler said as he tipped the brim of his hat back off his forehead.

Dani took in the sight of him with just a bit too much interest. Leather chaps were tied to his powerfully built thighs. The turquoise belt buckle forced her to notice his lean waist and move farther to take in the impressive width of his broad shoulders. His face was devoid of expression, like one of those granite sculptures from decades long past.

"If you're finished drinking yourself stupid, can we go?"

Dani was vaguely aware of the sound of an engine being started. "Oh no!" she yelped when she saw the Testarossa back out of the drive.

"Don't worry," Ty assured her as his steely hand reached out for her upper arm. "I brought along one of the men to drive your car back so we wouldn't have to come all the way out here tomorrow, when you sober up."

"Come back anytime," her friend said, before dissolving into a series of slurred chuckles.

"Thanks, Carol," Dani said somberly. The intimidating look of Ty's stiff, disapproving stance acted like an entire pot of coffee in her system. "Maybe Sandra would have been the lesser of two evils," she grumbled as Ty jerked her in the direction of the pickup parked by the curb. "You're hurting me!"

"Sorry," he said.

Dani didn't hear any regret in his tone. Chancing a peek at him through her lashes, she found herself enthralled by the masculine angles and sun-bronzed skin. Reluctantly she secretly acknowledged Ty's good looks and the allure of the soap-and-leather scent that wreaked havoc with her pulse. "I really should have taken my chances with Sandra."

"Why?" Ty asked as he held open the passenger door.

Squaring her shoulders, Dani looked up into the shimmering dark pools and said, "At least my aunt is consistent. She doesn't go rushing off without so much as a wave goodbye."

The corners of his mouth twitched slightly before turning up into a smug grin. Dani felt her blood pressure rising along with his apparent merriment.

"Is that why you didn't return any of my calls? You were angry that I left in a hurry and canceled our date?"

"Calls?" she asked in disbelief. "You didn't call, and it was *not* a date." Dani crossed her arms in front of her chest and glared up at him.

"I did call. Ask your aunt." Tyler helped her into the cab of the truck with as much dignity as he might have offered one of the ranch's cattle. She wound up sprawled half in and half out, with Tyler folding her legs at the knees in order to close the door.

Tyler eased himself behind the wheel, his weight forcing Dani's head to all but land in his lap. "Try and sit up, Danielle!'' he barked before throwing the car into gear.

Struggling against the centrifugal forces, she finally managed to right herself in the seat. Using the back of her hand, Dani brushed some of the strands of hair from her eyes. ''If you wouldn't have thrown me in here like a sack of feed, I wouldn't have ended up sprawled across the cab.''

''If you hadn't spent the day drinking yourself stupid at Carol's, I wouldn't have had to interrupt my day by driving all the way out here.''

''I didn't ask you to.''

''Did you think your uncle would come all this way?''

''Actually,'' Dani said as she took in a breath and tried to focus her blurred vision on the latch of the glove compartment, ''I think my uncle would gladly do anything I asked.''

''As long as Sandra let go of his leash long enough.''

''Whatever,'' she said, dismissively. ''And what was that crack about calling me?''

''I did call,'' he said in a deceptively soft tone. Even in her sluggish state, Dani could tell by the tightness of his grip on the wheel that Tyler's body was tensed from some emotion.

''Whatever you say,'' she countered, stiffening her spine in response to the taut set of his jaw.

''Do you always give in so easily?''

''Who said I was giving in?''

''You all but admitted you got my messages from Sandra.''

Dani let out a mirthless chuckle. "Think, Tyler. My aunt took great pleasure in telling me that you went off to do the bidding of some woman. Do you really think she would deliver messages that might spare me the evening ridicule that has tainted every meal since the day you left?"

"I didn't really think about it that way."

"Just for future reference, Sandra lives to make my life miserable."

"She did mention that you've been after them to fire me in my absence."

Dani felt her face grow warm. "I haven't found you terribly reliable as an employee."

Tyler reached out and captured her chin with his callused thumb and forefinger. Her breath caught in her throat as she looked into the depths of his warm brown eyes.

"Is it my employment record, or is it the fact that I went to do a lady a favor that ruffled your feathers?"

"I don't have feathers," she said as she slapped his hand away.

"No," he admitted reluctantly. "What you have is a dead sister and an intentionally set fire."

A shiver danced the full length of her spine. "Are you sure?"

"Am I sure the fire was intentional?"

Dani nodded.

"Absolutely."

"I still don't understand why someone would want to kill Jennifer."

Tyler ran his finger across the brim of his hat. "I'm convinced the answer is connected to the murder of your parents."

Dani cleared her throat. "But Stone killed my parents. He was tried and convicted." She twirled the ends of a few strands of hair between her fingers. "If he didn't kill my parents, why did he hang himself after the trial?"

She noticed that Tyler began to fidget in his seat and drum his thumbs against the wheel of the truck.

"Who knows?"

"What if Jen found something to indicate that he was innocent?"

"He was found guilty, Dani. Maybe he couldn't face a lifetime of bars and guards, so he just threw in the towel."

"Surely he could have found some way to prove his innocence. There were appeals—"

"Twenty years ago the court system wasn't as effective as it is now. Stone was a poor man. Poor men got a different version of justice."

"If that's true—" Dani paused as she felt her years of resolve beginning to melt "—four people have died for the same reason. But what's the reason?"

"Nothing we know about," Tyler said as he reached over to give her leg a gentle squeeze. "I think Jennifer was close to something. Have you had an opportunity to order another transcript?"

"It came yesterday."

"Does anyone know what you're doing?"

"Just Uncle Matt and Sandra. They signed for the courier."

"Did they say anything?"

"Sandra just wanted to know if I'd be taking the package back to Atlanta with me."

"Very hospitable."

"Very Sandra."

"Are you planning on going back soon?"

Dani wondered if she was imagining the strange tone in his voice. Was it possible that Tyler didn't want her to go home to Atlanta? "I've made arrangements to have all my books and equipment sent out. I'm going to convert one of the rooms upstairs to an office."

"My room?" Ty asked as he shook a cigarette from the crumpled pack on the dash. Dani watched transfixed as he rolled the filter on his tongue.

"No," she squeaked.

"Sandra said you were determined to get rid of me."

"I was."

"'Was,' meaning you've changed your mind?"

"Let's just say I'm granting you a probationary period."

Tyler laughed.

"Just where do you plan on putting all this junk!"

Dani let out a breath and counted to ten before speaking. "Put them upstairs, third door on the right."

"That's the sewing room!" Sandra shrieked.

"No one in this family sews," Dani countered.

"You could have asked me."

"I could have, couldn't I?"

"What's going on?" Matt asked as soon as he appeared in the hallway.

"Danielle has taken it upon herself to commandeer the sewing room."

"Taking up sewing?" Matt asked innocently.

"No. I needed someplace to set up my computer and store my reference books."

"You should be storing them in Atlanta," her aunt injected.

"Do say what's on your mind, Sandra," Dani offered with a saccharine smile.

"I don't understand why you've decided to stay here, when you've said yourself there was nothing here for you to do."

"I've changed my mind," Dani answered her aunt.

"You could have asked us before you just took it upon yourself to move in."

Dani turned and met her aunt's narrowed eyes. "I don't have to ask, Sandra. This house belongs to me. You are here on sufferance. If it weren't for Uncle Matt, I don't think I'd be quite so generous."

"Generous!" Sandra cackled. "I was the one who sacrificed to raise you. Matthew and I never had a day to ourselves thanks to you and your sister. Is this the thanks I get?"

"I've said thank-you more times than I can count."

"You always were as selfish as your mother." Sandra turned and marched up the stairs in a cloud of billowing chiffon.

"Sorry," Dani said to her uncle as she looped her arm through his. "You can take the rest of the stuff up," she told the workmen.

"Sandra isn't going to let this pass," Matt told her as his shoulders slumped forward.

"I know," Dani said. Standing on tiptoe, she placed a kiss on her uncle's wrinkled cheek. "I'll wait awhile and apologize."

"If you don't, there'll be hell to pay."

"Don't worry." Dani gave him a squeeze before watching him lumber down the hall, toward his stash of Scotch.

After giving the men a cool drink and a tip, Dani went up to survey the chaos. "Definitely needs some work," she said aloud. There were definitely too many boxes, and there was definitely too little shelf space. Emptying one of the boxes, she began to remove the pattern books from the built-ins. Dust and the outdated fashions attested to the fact that the items hadn't been touched in decades. With a pang of sorrow, she silently acknowledged that the sewing paraphernalia had belonged to her mother.

"Oh my," she whispered as she looked at the cover of one of the books. It featured a lounging robe that caused a strobelike image to appear in her mind. Superimposed over the pattern book was the vision from her dream. Feeling dizzy, Dani sucked in her breath, her heartbeat beginning to pound in her ears. Without taking her eyes off the picture, she groped behind her for someplace to sit, just as her legs began to give way. "She was wearing this in my dream."

"What in God's name are you doing now?"

Sandra's venomous voice cut through Dani's troubled thoughts.

"What?"

"I heard a crash and came to see what you'd destroyed now."

Numbly Dani looked behind her, noticing the small spray of broken glass on the polished wood. "I knocked over a glass. It must have been left by one of the deliverymen."

"I certainly hope you clean it up before someone gets hurt."

"Yes, Aunt Sandra."

Clutching the book close to her chest, Dani shook her head to try to organize her thoughts. Stepping down, she used her free hand to gingerly collect the slivers of glass. "The dream isn't real," she told herself. "If Mother did make this for herself, it isn't such a stretch for me to mix up that memory with the fantasy of my dream." Still, Dani couldn't bring herself to put the book down. After twenty-five years, she wanted to cling to anything even remotely connected to her mother.

She placed the pattern book on top of the box that contained her computer before going back to the task at hand. It took three boxes before she was able to clear the shelves.

"I've made a bigger mess," she said after surveying the cluttered floor. With her hands resting on her hips, she considered her options. "There's only one," she admitted after a full five minutes. "You have to carry this stuff up to the attic."

Dani knew she could set her computer up on the old treadle machine. Her printer would have to live on the floor, but first she would have to clear some floor space by carting some of the stuff into the dark and creepy attic. "Jen, I really miss you now!" she grunted as she lifted the first box. Her sister had never been afraid of the shadowy attic. Dani had been up there only once, when Jen and a friend had lured her there with the promise of candy. The older girls had blocked the door, leaving Dani trapped in the scary surroundings. Ironically, it was Sandra who had freed her that day. It was the only kind thing her aunt had ever done.

The trapdoor was in the bathroom. Dani had to put the box on the vanity and jump in order to reach the string dangling a few inches below the ceiling door. "Come on!" she grunted as she stretched her arm and groped for the string. "Yes!" she said as she finally reached and jerked on the string.

The door creaked open, revealing a set of iron steps, folded at the halfway point. Dani pulled the ladder down, testing the bottom step before she ventured up into the eaves.

"Be brave," she told herself as she reached the darkened space. Setting the box aside, she felt along the joist until she found the switch. A naked bulb in the center of the room cast more shadows than it did light. Careful to step only on the framing, Dani made her way over to a stack of boxes in the far corner. "What the heck?" she said as she took in the sight before her.

Placing her box on top of another, Dani examined the items arranged atop an empty crate inverted as a desk top. A hurricane lamp containing a nearly melted candle was nestled in the center of several file folders.

"Brock's Pass Sheriff's Department," she read aloud as she picked up the folder. The inside was empty. So was the one marked Coroner's Report. So was the folder marked AAA Detective Agency. Beneath the third empty file, Dani was stunned to find a tattered copy of the trial transcript.

"State of Montana v. Hayden Stone," she read. Leaning against a stack of boxes, Dani angled the page so that she could better make out the faded print. She was halfway through the first paragraph when her attention was diverted by the scent of soap and leather filling the air. Expecting Tyler, she turned in time to see a gloved hand cradling a white cloth close over her nose and mouth. Darkness came before she saw the face.

Chapter Five

She struggled to see through the bluish haze that blanketed her vision. Battling to lift her heavy arm, she tried to command her hand to move to her face in an attempt to wipe away the fog.

"It lives."

The sound of Tyler's voice had her instantly alert. Fear easily edged out confusion.

"Get away from me!"

Dani scooted backward several inches, only to have her retreat halted by a stack of weighted boxes. "I mean it, Cantrell!" she warned, forcing her eyes opened wide. "Aunt Sandra, call the sheriff!"

Her aunt let out an annoyed stream of breath and placed impatient hands in the vicinity of her waist. "*Do* try not to be melodramatic, Danielle. Your theatrics have brought this family nothing but trouble in the past."

"You don't understand! I was putting the sewing stuff away when—"

"Don't start your hysterics," Sandra cautioned with a threatening arch of a drawn-on eyebrow.

"But, Sandra!"

"Oh, good heavens!" Sandra grunted. "You probably just bumped your head. I'll see if Sam is available to check you out. He's busy at the stables, but if it will shut you up, I'll see if he has a minute or two."

"Sam?" Dani wailed at the disappearing form of her aunt. Feeling a tightness in her throat, her hands flew to her neck. Her eyes wide, she watched Tyler come closer.

"You're really scared, aren't you?"

"I swear, Cantrell," she said as her eyes narrowed at him, "one step closer and I'll scream my bloody head off!"

"Calm down!" he instructed. Taking in her trembling body and the raised red welts in a square around her tightly closed lips, Ty felt a sudden and fierce pang of concern creep into his consciousness. "Why are you so afraid of me?"

She appeared to tense at his question. "What did you do to me?"

"Me?"

He watched as she struggled to her feet. Feeling a strong desire to reach out and steady her, Tyler forced his clenched fists into the front pockets of his jeans.

She began to move toward the exit. "I saw you," she hissed.

"Saw me what?"

"Saw you put the cloth over my face."

Shaking his head, Tyler moved to block her route. He had no idea what she was talking about, but he knew he needed her. Most importantly, he needed her trust. "I don't know what happened up here—"

"Like hell."

"Now, Danielle," he said as he reached for her, only to have his hands swatted away. He made no move to touch her again. It wasn't necessary. Danielle had literally worked her way into the corner of the shadowy attic.

"Please let me leave."

The slight tremor in her voice stabbed at his gut. She reminded him of a small animal caught in a trap. He just couldn't understand how he had become the trapper in her mind. "I don't understand why you think I had something to do with whatever happened to you."

"Yeah, right!"

"Talk to me, Dani."

He watched the play of emotion in her eyes, saw the fear and confusion as clearly as if she'd spoken. The realization that this woman was getting to him was almost as disconcerting as having her accuse him of covering her face with a cloth.

"If it wasn't you—"

"It wasn't."

"Lord, Tyler..." Dani expelled his name on a breath and raked her slender fingers through her hair.

He wanted to gather her close to him, but he knew the time wasn't right.

"Tell me what happened."

She met his gaze. "If it wasn't you, then someone sure made a point of making me think it was."

"Start from the beginning," he urged, struggling to keep the exasperation out of his voice.

"I came up here to put a few things away when I found that."

"A stack of boxes and an old candle?"

"There were other things there, too."

"What other things?"

"Jennifer's things, I think."

"Clothes?" he asked as he took a step closer to her. His hand reached out and gently cradled her elbow, steering her back toward the teetering pile.

"Not clothes. Stuff that had to do with the trial."

His hand traveled up to grip her shoulder. With his heartbeat increasing, Tyler told himself it was the topic of discussion that was causing it, not the fascinating fragrance clinging to each strand of her hair.

"What kind of stuff?" His voice cracked slightly, but she didn't seem to notice. That knowledge only added to the tightness in his stomach.

His other hand went to her other shoulder, and he tugged her toward him. She felt soft beneath his grip, and he silently decided not to question his actions. Her head fell back as her eyes met his. Her pale green eyes caught and held the faint light, turning them into lush, shimmering pools. The sound of her breathing fanned the fires burning deep in the pit of his gut. His thumb found its way to her chin, then ventured farther, to the gentle slope of her lower lip.

His heart was pounding in his ears, and Tyler knew it was time to decide. He also knew there could be no other decision. Tentatively his hand fanned out against her cheek, leaving his thumb to rest against her slightly parted lips. Her breath was warm where it spilled over his hand. His eyes fixed on her mouth as his fantasies began to mingle with the reality of being so close to perfection.

"Tyler, I . . ."

Tyler wondered if she knew how incredibly sexy her voice was. He doubted it.

She moved closer to him, until he could feel the outline of her body molding against him. Restraint was becoming a foreign concept.

When her tongue flicked out to moisten her lower lip, Tyler followed the movement with the pad of his thumb. His action caused her mouth to open farther, and her hands moved up and captured fistfuls of his shirt. When she lifted up on tiptoe, Tyler swallowed the groan in his throat. The heat in his stomach had moved lower, inspiring a whole new array of fantasies.

"Tyler."

He heard his name at about the same time he felt her begin to pull away. He desperately wanted to feel her hands on him, to continue this sweet exploration for the next several hours.

"Tyler."

"Not yet," he pleaded.

"Listen!" she insisted, tugging free.

Her face was flushed, effectively erasing the faint traces of red he'd noticed around her mouth.

"That's got to be Aunt Sandra!"

"Great timing," Tyler groaned as he listened to the unmistakable sound of footsteps climbing the attic ladder.

She didn't have time to consider what had nearly happened between them. Not when she caught sight of Sam Brightwood following on her aunt's heels.

"Why did you bring him here?" she groaned at her aunt. "I thought inviting him for dinner was a bit much, but this!"

"Don't put on airs, Danielle. You were the one on the verge of hysteria, so I brought Sam."

"He's an ambulance driver, Sandra, not a doctor."

"He's the best I could do."

"Look," Sam began, in a small, quiet voice, "I told your aunt I didn't think this was such a smart idea."

"You were right," Dani assured him. Squaring her shoulders, she refused to be distracted by Tyler's smoldering brown eyes. "I don't need a ride, Sam."

"Danielle!" her aunt yelped. One heavily jeweled hand flew to her mouth.

"Forgive me, but in light of the past, I would think you'd have known better than to bring him within ten feet of me."

Her aunt grabbed a handful of the slender man's shirtsleeve, dragging him forward. "See, I told you she was hysterical."

"I am not hysterical!" Dani realized too late that her shrill voice had done little to further her cause. "Someone placed a rag with some sort of chemical over my face."

Tyler's expression crumbled into deep furrows of concern. "You thought it was me?"

"He smelled like you!"

"Smelled?" Sandra derisively.

"Soap and leather," Dani continued, blindly reaching out in Tyler's direction. Her hand closed on his bicep, and her breath caught in her throat as she felt the corded muscle beneath her hand. Her eyes moved from face to face. Sam refused to meet her gaze. Sandra glared at her with open hostility. Tyler's expression was impossible to read. She was beginning to wonder if perhaps she had imagined the events of the recent past.

"What are you talking about?" Ty asked, his hands gripping her shoulders.

Dani stumbled over her thoughts, distracted by the faint outline of the silky brown hair covering his chest.

"I was standing with my back to the stairway. I had just begun to look through the stuff I found on top of that box when I smelled soap and leather. I turned, expecting to find you, when a hand holding a white square of cloth closed over my mouth."

"What did it smell like?"

Since the question came from Sam, Dani rolled her eyes in annoyance. "I told you. Soap and leather."

"No." Sam, flanked by her aunt, shuffled over to the area where Dani and Tyler stood toe-to-toe. "Did the cloth smell like something?"

Dani thought for a second before shaking her head. "No. But whatever was on that rag worked quickly. I didn't even have a chance to look at his face when—"

"Oh, please!" Sandra said with an exasperated breath. "Your imagination has always been flawed. When you were a child, we overlooked your little quirk as an amusement. Now that you're an adult, it is neither a quirk nor amusing."

"Shut up and go downstairs, Sandra," Tyler growled.

After one last baleful stare, Sandra stomped from the attic. Sam shuffled his weight from booted foot to booted foot. His head remained bowed.

"Why did you ask her about the smell?" Tyler demanded of the other man.

"Ether has a really distinctive smell."

"Then it wasn't ether. What else could have caused her to pass out?"

Sam scratched his head as he thought.

Dani was not the least bit interested in anything Sam had to say. "This is stupid, Tyler. He's not a doctor, for God's sake! He volunteers for the ambulance corps!"

"Calm down," Tyler said as he ran his hands up and down her arms. "Give me some ideas, Brightwood. What kind of drug might have that effect on her?"

"Any skin reactions?" Sam asked.

"There's redness around her mouth."

"What?" Dani said, horrified. "What's around my mouth?"

"The outline of a square." He turned to the other man. "Take a look, Sam."

"Take a hike, Sam!" Dani countered, moving back as Sam moved forward. The fingers of one of Dani's hands moved to her face, and she did feel a slight imperfection on the surface of her skin. "A square? From the cloth?" she asked Tyler.

"It's not very dark, but it's the general shape and size of a folded handkerchief."

Sam stroked his chin. "It could be some sort of alcohol-based chemical. That would irritate the skin, but not form blisters."

"Any ideas?" Tyler asked.

"Some sort of chemical used in pesticides, maybe some sort of cleanser or polish. Most of your household products have an alcohol base."

"How would you know?" Dani demanded suspiciously.

"I got my undergraduate degree in chemical engineering."

"You?"

"Do you think you could stop taking potshots at the guy, Dani? He's trying to be of help."

"Thank you, Mr. Cantrell," she returned hotly, folding her arms in front of her chest and glaring at the both of them. "*You* are a chemical engineer?"

"Yep," Sam admitted with a blush.

He looked contrite, all right, but Dani was not quite ready to forgive him his trespasses.

"Did your face burn when it contacted the chemical?"

Rolling her eyes, Dani suddenly wondered at what point she had lost all her faculties. Here she was in the attic of her own home, in the company of the man who had killed her innocence, and she was calmly discussing the properties of various chemicals.

"Sam," she began through tight, thinned lips, "I appreciate your little attempt at helping out, but it's just a tad too little, and years too late."

"Ignore her," Tyler inserted. "Can we find out exactly what was used on her?"

"Blood test, maybe."

"Excuse me, boys, but you both seem to have lost sight of the fact that I'm not some dumb cow that the two of you can discuss like the weather. And what good would a blood test do at this point?"

Tyler and Sam exchanged impatient expressions. Tyler then said, "If we can find out what was used on you, maybe we can find out who used it."

"And what do I do? Walk into a doctor's office and calmly tell him I'm there because I've been sniffing the furniture polish?"

"Do you want to try and find out who did this?" Tyler countered.

"No," she drawled at him sarcastically, "I think ignorance is bliss. Of course I want to know who did this."

"I think I'll be heading on back to my place... if there's nothing else you need," Sam said.

"Don't let me keep you," Dani said curtly, just before Sam cracked the back of his head on a joist. She stifled her giggle.

"Do you have to browbeat the poor guy?"

"Poor guy!" Dani's fists balled at her sides. "Sam Brightwood is slime."

"Ten years have passed since then. Maybe it's time for you to lighten up."

"Me? You don't know what you're talking about, Cantrell." She went to move past him, but Tyler only reached out and captured her upper arm. "What now?"

"Why are you so blasted angry at me? All I want to do is try to make some sense out of what happened here this afternoon."

"Tyler..." Dani said as she tilted her head back in order to meet his eyes. The expression she found there simply melted her anger. She saw warmth and kindness, two things she desperately needed. "So, I'll go into Brock's Pass and get a blood test."

"Good girl," he said with a wink.

Dani punched him in the kidney.

"What'd ya do that for?"

"I don't like being called 'girl.'"

"You could have just said so," he grumbled as he rubbed his lower back.

"Don't be such a baby!" she told him. "I didn't hit you that hard, and you're at least twice my size."

"It still hurt."

"So pout. That's certainly adult behavior."

"When did you become this abusive feminist?" he asked as he renewed his hold on her upper arms.

"I'm not abusive," she countered, feeling her pulse rate begin to increase as his eyes dropped lower. It didn't help that she seemed transfixed on the vast expanse of his chest, not to mention the corded muscles at his lean waist.

"But..." He caught her chin between his thumb and forefinger. "You are a feminist."

"I am not now, nor have I ever been, a member of the Communist Party." Tyler laughed in spite of his dire injury. He pulled her against him, where Dani was treated to the feel of his body as it rose and fell with deep laughter. He was warm, and she felt decidedly comfortable inside the blanket of his arms. She could feel his heart beating as erratically as her own.

"This isn't going to get you a blood test," he warned her as his laughter stilled and his hand laced through the strands of her hair.

"Meaning?" Dani asked as she looked up to meet his eyes.

Tyler shook his head sadly, but a definite smile curved the corners of his mouth. "Blood test, *then* we play house."

Dani slapped at him and lowered her head for fear he would see the faint blush warming her cheeks. "I don't play house."

"Then we'll play apartment," Tyler countered with a swat to her backside.

She was halfway to the stairway when she remembered the makeshift desk. "I wonder how they knew about the stuff," she mused.

"What stuff?"

"The stuff that I found laid out when I got here. The stuff that compelled someone to drug me in order for them to get at it."

"What kind of stuff?"

"It must have been Jen's," Dani decided. "There was a tattered copy of the trial transcript. Then a few empty file folders."

"What were they for?"

"One was labeled 'sheriff's report,' the other was the coroner's report, I think. I don't remember the other one. I guess Jen worked up here before she hooked up with you."

The expression on Tyler's face froze as if suddenly turned to stone.

"What?"

Tyler's eyes looked past her into the dark recesses of the attic.

"Tyler, what is it?"

"Those things couldn't have belonged to your sister."

"How can you be so sure?"

"They were reported lost almost immediately after the trial, twenty years ago."

Tyler gently cradled her elbow as they came down from the attic. As they descended to the first floor, she saw her aunt and Sam seated in the kitchen, and couldn't wait to leave the house. She and Tyler quietly slipped out the front door and hightailed it for the car, making a clean getaway.

"How do you get away with ordering Sandra around like that?"

"Like what?" Ty asked as he shifted the car.

"Like in the attic. I was preoccupied at the time, but I've never known my aunt to take orders from anyone."

Ty turned his head to face her, but Dani was careful to avoid any direct eye contact. Parts of her body still tingled from the memory of their brief but pleasurable encounter in the attic.

When he remained silent, Dani prodded him. "Well? Are you going to tell me, or do we have to play twenty questions?"

He laughed. "You are one of the most dangerous creatures known to mankind, Danielle."

"What's that supposed to mean?" Whatever it was, Dani didn't think it sounded like a flattering assessment of her character.

"You're an intelligent, angry woman. Very dangerous stuff."

"I'm not angry!"

"Then why do you refuse to give Sam the benefit of the doubt? He isn't eighteen anymore." Tyler reached out and stroked her thigh, just above her knee. "Neither are you, for that matter."

"You're out of line, Cantrell."

"It's all right for you to grill me about Sandra, but your interpersonal dynamics are off-limits, huh?"

Dani let out a disgusted breath and angled it toward her bangs. "No. We were talking about Sandra, not Sam."

"I'm talking about Sam."

"Then I'm not talking."

"Very adult behavior, Dani."

They rode the rest of the way to Brock's Pass in silence. He tried not to watch her in his peripheral vision, but that proved to be a futile task. Tyler mentally acknowledged his skillful manipulation of this beautiful woman he had held in his arms. He had known that the mere mention of Sam Brightwood's name would divert her probing questions. Her passion provided a second weapon for his arsenal.

"MAKE A FIST."

"Given my company, that won't be too difficult," Dani told the matronly lab technician.

The woman looked past the glass enclosure of the lab and spotted the tall blond man pacing in the waiting area. "I wouldn't go hitting that one. No, ma'am! He's too cute to hit."

"Spend some time with him."

"I'm game if he is."

Dani smiled at the woman, who had obviously been staring down too many test tubes, if she couldn't see what an arrogant, overbearing, incredibly sexy heel Tyler was. "Why did I include incredibly sexy?" Dani mumbled.

"Excuse me? Bend your arm up. We're done."

"Forget it," Dani said as she placed her finger at the bend of her arm and applied pressure.

"Does Dr. Peters need to see you back in his office?"

"No."

"Then take this copy to the cashier on the first floor." The woman went about labeling the vial of blood, and Dani was all too willing to leave.

"Did it hurt?"

"Of course it hurt," she said, careful to keep her back straight and her steps brisk and purposeful.

"Do you want me to kiss it and make it better?"

Dani stopped short, grabbing a handful of Tyler's shirt and pulling him to one side of the tiled corridor. "Forget what happened earlier. That kind of thing just screws up a working relationship."

Tyler cocked his head to one side and regarded her. "Interesting word choice."

"Get your brain out of your pants!" she said seethingly between clenched teeth. "I didn't say that correctly. What I meant to say was that we need to have a functional working relationship and that won't happen if we...if you...It just doesn't..."

"I'm not going to forget that I was about to kiss you, Dani." His head dipped fractionally. "I don't think I could even if I wanted to. And I don't want to."

Swallowing, Dani let go of his shirt and tried to quell the fluttering in her stomach. The early-evening air danced over her skin as they emerged from the small medical center on the far edge of town. When Ty took her elbow, Dani didn't bother to put up a fight. She wasn't one to fight the inevitable. *All anyone had to do was ask Aunt Sandra.*

"How about dinner?"

"What did you have in mind?" she asked without looking at him.

"The luncheonette?"

"I'd rather starve."

"Now how did I know that?" Tyler taunted as he steered her in the direction of the Testarossa. "There's a pretty decent Mexican joint over near Beaumont."

"That's almost an hour and a half from here!"

"Are you going to die of hunger before then?"

"I didn't mean that," Dani said huffily. "I'm just not used to driving all over creation for a flaming plate of food."

"I don't think they do flambé at Jose's."

"Very funny, Cantrell. Is everything a joke with you?"

"No."

The hum of the high-performance engine was barely audible in the compact passenger compartment. Try as she might, Dani's thoughts seemed to careen in Tyler's direction at every turn. She noticed the way his chambray shirt hugged the definition of muscle across his broad chest. She noticed the way his well-worn jeans outlined his powerful thighs. Even the unruly mass of blond hair intrigued her feminine senses. *What has gotten into me?* she wondered.

"What's gotten into you?" Tyler asked, giving her a guilty start.

"Me? Nothing."

"You're as tense as a calf about to be branded."

"Thank you for comparing me to livestock. I can't tell you what that does for my ego." Dani toyed with a strand of her hair.

"I didn't mean it that way, so you don't have to get huffy."

"Fine," she returned with a sigh. She didn't like this man providing commentary on her demeanor. It was unnerving.

Twisting in her seat, Dani regarded his chiseled profile in the waning shadows of daylight. "I'd like to have an answer to how you get away with ordering Sandra around."

Tyler shrugged and tapped his thumbs against the steering wheel.

"Not good enough," she insisted. "There's more to all this than you've let on, and I'm no longer blinded by concern for my sister, or by mourning. I would like to know how you were able to work your way into my family."

"By invitation."

Dani noted a small twitch of his jaw muscle and wondered if it was some sort of indicator that he was avoiding the truth. "Could you be a little more elaborate with your response?"

"Your sister found me and asked me to work on the Circle B while she and I reviewed the circumstances of your parents' murder."

"I can understand Jennifer doing that. I can't understand the fact that you, obviously, have Sandra wrapped around your finger." Dani wished she could will the daylight to remain long enough for her to see the play of emotions across his face. She got no cooperation from nature. The interior of the car was dark, making it impossible for her to see anything more than the outline of his ruggedly handsome face.

"I think you're giving me too much credit."

The headlights of another car split the distance between them with a bluish strip of bright light.

"C'mon, Cantrell! You say jump and my aunt asks how high. What do you have to lord over her—"

The blare of an emergency siren silenced Dani, forcing her to turn even farther in her seat to peer out through the severely angled back window.

Strobelike red and blue beams closed the distance between the cars.

"Wonderful," Tyler muttered as he eased his foot off the accelerator and steered the car toward the shoulder of the deserted strip of highway.

"Were you speeding?"

"No."

"Then why are we being pulled over?"

"I reckon we're about to find out."

The sound of a car door closing filtered in as Tyler lowered his window. Dani could hear the crackle of a police radio mingling with the sound of heavy footsteps meeting the gravel shoulder. "It's Sheriff Cassidy," Dani said as she watched the rotund man lumbering toward them.

"Just what we need," Tyler said, just as the stench of chewing tobacco reached her nose.

Cassidy spit loudly and then crouched to shine his flashlight directly into Dani's eyes.

"Miss Baylor," Cassidy drawled through the bulge in his lower lip. "Didn't see you there."

"Sheriff," she said stiffly as she cupped her hand over her eyes to shield them from the offensive light.

"Is everything all right?"

"I'm afraid I don't understand your question," Dani told him.

"I recognized the car, and I was afraid Cantrell here had taken it out without permission."

Dani noticed Tyler gripping the wheel with white knuckles.

"Why would you think that?" she asked.

"Well . . ." Cassidy turned his pudgy head and spit yet again. "Cantrell isn't too well-known."

Tyler's eyebrows drew together, and Dani could almost feel the anger surging through his veins.

Cassidy continued, "I know your sister was mighty particular about this here car. She's probably turning in her grave, knowing you're letting a stranger drive it."

Placing her hand on the console that separated them, Dani leaned toward Tyler. "I don't think you need to concern yourself with what my sister may or may not be doing in her grave."

Cassidy's face appeared to mirror the red of his emergency light. "You may want to be a bit more particular about the company you keep, Miss Baylor."

Dani didn't like being told what to do. She found it especially distasteful when the command came from a man whose pants usually revealed enough of his rear end to cause nausea. "I'm sorry you wasted your time, Sheriff."

"It's my job to make sure the likes of a man like Cantrell don't take advantage of a lady such as yourself."

"Mr. Cantrell is my employee, Sheriff."

"Is there a problem here?" Tyler barked.

Unfortunately, the sheriff seemed to bristle at Tyler's voice, and Dani sensed they were headed for a minor disaster.

"Don't give me any of your lip, boy," Cassidy warned.

"Boy?" Tyler repeated in a dull, even timbre.

"Don't take that tone with me," Cassidy replied.

"Sheriff," Dani said, imploringly. "I realize that you thought it was necessary to stop the car. Since you now know that everything is fine, I don't think we need to bother ourselves with personality conflicts."

Cassidy shifted and tapped his fingers against the handle of his nightstick. Dani felt the waves of hostility bouncing back and forth between the two stoic men.

"I had another reason for stopping the car," Cassidy said as he tugged at the waistband of his uniform. The three of them were still at eye level. "I hear you had some trouble out your way this afternoon."

"Yes, we had—"

"Nothing happened," Tyler said, interrupting her. His hand closed over the top of her knee, and he applied enough pressure to communicate his desire that she keep her mouth closed.

"Is that right?" Cassidy pressed.

Dani felt torn. Lying to a police officer went against her nature. Still, this man had done nothing to earn her respect. "I had a minor accident in the attic," she responded after a short pause.

"Accident?" Cassidy scoffed. "That ain't the way I heard it."

"Who did you hear it from?" Tyler asked.

"I wasn't talking to you, boy," Cassidy said.

"Actually," Dani began as she leaned her upper body into Tyler in the hope that she could diffuse the current of animosity passing between the men, "I would be interested to know who told you about my accident."

Cassidy stood slowly and made a production out of spitting yet again.

"Sheriff?"

"I don't recall just now," he said as he lifted his hat and scratched the top of his head.

Dani's nose was assailed by the odor of whatever vile ointment he had used to slick down the thin strands of his hair. "What do you mean, you don't recall?" Dani asked.

"Yes, Bubba," Tyler added. "Do you expect us to believe that you are so overworked that you can't remember the source of your information?"

"Don't push me," Cassidy snapped.

"I'm certain that was not his intent." It was her turn to squeeze Tyler's leg.

He ignored her silent communication.

"I'm just curious," Tyler insisted.

"Too much curiosity ain't healthy—for either one of you." On that cryptic note, Cassidy turned and walked back toward his squad car.

"What was that all about?"

Tyler didn't respond. He pounded the car into gear and tore off the shoulder, filling the car with cool air from the opened window.

After regaining her position in the seat, Dani gaped at the furious expression marring his features. "What has gotten into you?"

"Cassidy."

"Why are you letting him get to you?"

Tyler shifted into second, very nearly giving her whiplash in the process. "That useless cretin!"

Dani swallowed at the fury tainting each syllable as it passed across his lips. "I don't exactly like him, either, but I don't let him get to me."

"He doesn't call you boy."

"Tyler." She said his name softly, hoping to improve his mood before the speedometer reached one hundred. "Cassidy is a jerk. Don't give him the satisfaction of making you angry."

"Doesn't it bother you that he knows what goes on inside your house?"

Dani sucked in a breath and let it out slowly. "It doesn't make me happy. I think it's just one of the hazards of living in a small community."

They rode in silence for several miles as Dani pondered the bizarre incidents of the preceding twenty-four hours. Very little about her life seemed to make sense these days. "Why would someone go to all the trouble of drugging me, just to remove the files in the attic?"

"Who knew you were going to the attic?"

Dani felt her eyebrows draw together as she thought. "No one. That's what's so weird about all this. I had no plans to go into the attic until I realized I wouldn't have enough room for my equipment in the sewing room."

"Who was in the house just before you went up?"

"Aunt Sandra and Uncle Matt. Lupe was in the kitchen, I think. The delivery guys left about twenty minutes before I found the book."

"Hold it! What book?"

"Just an old pattern book."

"Try again," Tyler told her. "What was it about the book that caused that little vibration in your voice?"

"It was my mother's," she said.

"And?"

"And I think I recognized the robe on the cover."

"And?"

"And nothing."

Dani was glad when he opted to concentrate on the road instead of the incidents leading up to her ascent into the attic. There was just no way anyone could have known she was going into the attic. She hadn't known it herself.

"They don't have curbside service."

Dani started at the sound of his voice. Blinking, she was surprised to discover that they had parked in front of a Spanish-style building. The sound of guitar music brought with it the scent of spicy food.

Tyler reached her just as she placed her foot on the paved surface of the lot. His hand captured her arm, and he gently pulled her to a standing position.

"Hungry?" he asked as they entered the boisterous interior of the building. Dani could barely hear him over the animated conversations at the bar.

"Yes!" she yelled over the noise.

A woman dressed in a brightly-colored costume came toward them, clutching some menus to her ample bosom. Dani noted a flicker of recognition in her dark eyes as she greeted them. The woman didn't give Dani more than a cursory nod of acknowledgment.

They were taken through several small dining rooms to a glass-enclosed area toward the rear of the building. Dani took her seat and accepted the menu thrust into her lap.

"I'll send Linda over for your order."

"Thanks, Meg," Tyler said as he offered the buxom woman a smile that even caused Dani's heart to skip a beat.

"I take it you're something of a regular."

Tyler shifted slightly as he removed his Stetson and tossed it on the chair next to him. "I drop in every now and again."

Dani watched as his dark eyes danced with the flicker of the candle flame in the center of their table.

"Here you go." Yet another festively dressed woman with a more-than-ample bosom placed a ceramic pitcher next to the candle. "I'll be back shortly for your order."

Tyler lifted the pitcher as soon as the woman had left. He poured sangria into glasses and pushed one over to her. Dani quickly grabbed the glass and brought it to her lips. The fruity wine was warm as it slid down her throat.

"Easy, Dani," Tyler said through his smile.

Self-consciously she lowered the glass. Only then did she realize she had downed more than half the contents in a single gulp. Heat tinged her cheeks, and she knew she was blushing like some lovesick teenager. She looked up to find him staring at her, his head tilted to one side.

"You look a lot like your mother."

"Thank you," she said. "How do you know what my mother looked like?"

Tyler shook his head. The action caused his hair to reflect the light from the flame. "I saw a picture of her. It was taken right around the time she died."

The waitress returned for their order and made notes on their selections.

Running her finger around the rim of the glass, Dani spoke. "How do you think Sheriff Cassidy found out about the attic incident?"

He shrugged. "It had to be someone from the house."

"I don't think Sandra would say anything. She isn't big on airing family matters. Uncle Matt doesn't usually go in for gossip. Lupe would bite off her own tongue before she'd repeat anything she heard around the house. That pretty much takes care of everyone but you and me."

"You're forgetting Sam Brightwood."

Dani stiffened at the sound of his name. "You're right. I wonder what he was doing at the Circle B, anyway."

"Looking at one of the mares."

"What idiot would let that man look at our livestock?"

"Right here," Tyler said, lifting one hand to shoulder height.

"Why would you do such a thing?"

"The man's educated, and one hell of a horseman. The animal needed attention."

"The man is an animal. I won't permit you to use him to evaluate our livestock."

Tyler's expression grew hard and still, as if each feature were carved in granite. "You won't permit?"

Dani matched his stiff tone. "No, I won't."

He took a long sip from his glass, and his eyes narrowed to fierce-looking slits. "Don't even think about telling me what to do when it comes to the ranch, Danielle. Or anything else, for that matter."

"You're the foreman, I own the ranch. You seem to have forgotten that fact."

Dani matched him glare for glare as the waitress deposited platters of steaming, pungent food around the table.

"Will there be anything else?"

"No," they answered in unison.

Her appetite was fading under the intensity of his dark stare. *I'm not going to let you know that, though,* she thought as she lifted her fork. She ate the first few bites without tasting anything, still wondering if she'd be able to force the food past the lump of frustration caught in her throat. Several minutes of tense silence only heightened her awareness of the man seated across from her. She felt an odd mixture of anger and sadness. His arrogance made her mad, yet the realization that he was upset with her carried with it an odd sort of discomfort. *Why do I care if he likes me or not?* she wondered.

"Pass the guacamole," he requested.

Dani complied, lifting the small bowl and directing it toward him. His hand closed over hers. His touch seared through her skin to ignite a fire that burned quickly toward the pit of her stomach. His eyes met and held hers above the flicker of the candle.

"Can we call a truce?"

"I suppose," she hedged, trying not to become completely mesmerized by the seductive qualities of his deep voice.

"Instead of battling each other, don't you think we could better spend our energies trying to figure out what's happening?"

"Of course," she said, schooling her voice into light, even syllables.

"Good," he said before taking a bite of food.

"Why would Sam discuss what happened in the attic with Sheriff Cassidy?"

"I wouldn't have the first clue," Tyler admitted. "He doesn't usually talk unless his daddy gives him a script."

Dani gave a reluctant nod. "Then I think we've narrowed it down to telepathic communication."

He smiled. The display of white teeth set against his deeply tanned skin caused a fluttering in her stomach.

"I don't think that's the answer, but it may be the best we can do until we get the results of your blood work."

"What happens then?"

"Once we know what was used, we can start looking for who had access to the substance."

"Sounds about as promising as looking for a needle in a haystack," Dani said with a pout.

"Now you really look like your mother," he observed.

"If you only saw a photograph, how do you know her facial expressions?"

Immediately he broke eye contact and pretended to study the remnants of his dinner.

"Tyler? How is it you're so well versed regarding my mother?"

"It isn't important," he said as he lifted his head. His eyes seemed shrouded in secrecy, which only piqued her interest.

"Yes, it is. Tell me how you know so much about my mother."

Tyler looked at her with weary eyes. "I did meet her once, when I was a kid. We used to watch her when I was little."

"We who?"

"It isn't important, Dani. Trust me."

"It's important to me," she assured him, reaching out to pat the back of his hand.

Tyler withdrew from her touch.

"Why are you so jumpy all of a sudden?"

"Let's just forget this and focus on this afternoon."

Dani grinned at the boyish shuffling of his feet beneath the table. "Tell me what you were doing watching my mother, and I'll drop it."

"It's not important. Forget I said anything."

"I'm not going to forget it. You can't make a statement like that and then refuse to explain it."

"I can and I did," he told her, a bit too emphatically.

"What's the big deal here? So you and some other little boy had fun when you were kids, following my mother around? She was a striking young woman. It's nothing to be embarrassed about."

"Then let's drop it."

"Tell me, and I'll drop it."

"Trust me, Dani, you don't want to know."

"Trust me," she countered, "I have to know now. Your evasiveness has made me curious."

"Leave it alone," he said, more firmly.

"Are you afraid I'll make fun of you for having a crush on my mother? Is that it?"

"No."

Grasping his hand, Dani tugged gently in order to get him to look her in the eye. "Tell me, Tyler. I promise I won't make fun of you."

"It isn't what you think."

"I'm not going to think anything if you'll just tell me."

"You're not going to let this go, are you?"

"Nope."

He leaned forward, bracing his elbows on the table, and captured her hand between his. It took several seconds for him to formulate his next words.

"We used to follow your mother."

"Why?"

"She was having an affair with Hayden Stone."

Chapter Six

"He said what?"

Dani slumped against the chair and raked her hand through her hair. "He said they were having an affair," she told Carol.

"How would Tyler know such a thing?"

Dani rose and paced behind her makeshift desk. "He was evasive on that point. But, apparently, he lived in Brock's Pass for a short time when he was younger."

Carol leaned against the shelving. "I don't remember Tyler."

Dani nodded. "Neither do I. But he said that he moved when he was eleven. Right after my parents were killed."

Carol's features contorted in deep concentration. "Now that you mention it, I do remember a woman named Cantrell. I think she worked at Quigley's."

"Even if that part of his story is true, what would an eleven-year-old boy be doing following my mother and Stone around?"

Carol shrugged. "Maybe he had a crush on her. My oldest has a thing for the dental hygienist. He's the only eight-year-old I know who insists he be monitored for the possibility of periodontal disease."

Dani smiled then, feeling some of the tension leave her sleep-deprived body. "I must be getting paranoid," she admitted. "I'm not even sure he's right. An eleven-year-old is hardly an appropriate judge of whether two people are romantically involved."

"Have you asked your uncle? Or Sandra?"

Dani made a sound that was dangerously like a snort. "Sandra wouldn't tell me anything, even if I did ask. And you know Uncle Matt. He's oblivious to everything."

"There must be some way for you to find out if Tyler is telling the truth."

"I'm hoping there's something in the trial transcript," she said. "If my mother was having an affair with her killer, surely it would have been brought out in court."

"What would have?"

Both women started and turned in the direction of the doorway. Tyler filled the small space. His hair was damp, as was his shirt. His dusty hat dangled between his thumb and forefinger, near his thigh. It was obvious from his stern expression that he didn't approve of her discussing the trial with Carol. Dani was beginning to wonder at his behavior, among other things.

"I was just telling Carol about the little bomb you dropped on me last night."

His dark eyes volleyed between the two women. He didn't know Carol well, but he did know she was a lifelong resident of Brock's Pass. That alone was enough to make him suspicious. Though she would have been Dani's age at the time of the murder, she could still have guilty knowledge. He decided to reserve forming an opinion on her until he'd had a chance to dig into her background.

"May I speak to you for a moment?" he asked.

Dani nodded reluctantly. Carol smiled and announced she would be in the kitchen with Lupe, should Dani need her for anything.

He noticed that sadness still clouded Dani's pretty eyes. He also sensed hesitation, and wondered again if he'd made the right decision in telling her about the affair.

As soon as the sound of Carol's footsteps faded to mere echoes, he moved toward her. She smelled of flowers, and seemed to watch his every move like some sort of cautious animal. He knew he should ignore the way the fabric of her clothing clung to each sensual curve of her body.

"Do you think that's smart?"

"What?"

"Bringing Carol into this," he explained in even tones.

"I'm not even sure I know what *this* is." Moving closer to the sill, Dani swallowed nervously.

"Someone killed your sister. I'd think you would want to protect your friend by not dragging her into this mess."

Dani pivoted on the ball of her bare foot. "You don't think . . ."

He shrugged. "I'm not sure what to think. I only know that there's something about your parents' death that has fatal consequences for anyone delving too deeply into it."

"But Carol isn't delving. She's a friend. Someone I can talk to." She looked up at him through the veil of her lashes. "She's not going to repeat what I said, and besides—" Dani squared her shoulders and dipped her head back farther "—your little revelation about my mother is hard for me to accept."

He felt his jaw tighten at the pain he heard in her voice. "I know it isn't something you wanted to hear, but I swear to you, it's the truth."

He hoped the rational part of her believed him. He felt certain the memory of her mother was important. Judging by her stiff posture, he guessed Dani wasn't too thrilled to have him tarnish that memory. He could only hope that the death of her sister was equally significant.

"I still don't understand how you know all this. You were eleven years old."

His eyes left her face and fixed on the scene beyond the window. "You'll just have to trust me, Dani."

She placed her hands on her hips. It was difficult not to follow the motion with his eyes.

"It's really hard for me to trust someone I know absolutely nothing about."

"Then don't," he returned easily. It was a gamble—a risk. He prayed it worked. "But I think you're taking one hell of a chance by involving Carol."

"She's my friend."

"And Jennifer was your sister," he reminded her quietly.

There it was again—that look that knotted his gut. How, he wondered, could she appear so strong on the outside, when her eyes told him she was crumbling on the inside? He didn't know whether to hug her or keep pressing.

"You're scaring me, Tyler."

"I've—"

The phone interrupted him with its high-pitched ring.

"Hello," Dani said into the receiver.

"Tyler Cantrell, please."

It was a woman. Dani considered asking her name, but decided against it and handed him the phone. She felt it was necessary to give him privacy; plus she noted an urgent edge to the woman's tone.

"I understand," he said as he turned away from Dani. "I'll have to call you back. This isn't a good time for me." There was a brief pause before he said, "I know. I know. I will."

After dropping the receiver on the cradle, Tyler placed his hat on his head and began moving toward the door. "Think about what I said. Think about who you take into your confidence."

Those words reverberated in her mind hours later, when she was steering the Testarossa toward Brock's Pass. While she wasn't convinced by Tyler's argument, she wasn't willing to jeopardize Carol's safety, either. She needed to read through the transcript, but before doing so, Dani had decided to follow up on what she'd seen in the attic. She knew Tyler would probably be furious if he knew what she was about to do, but she needed some independent corroboration. Once she had that, she knew she could give Tyler what he wanted from her—trust.

The sheriff's office was nearly deserted. She did find the well-endowed Bambi at her desk. Several of the woman's fingertips were dotted with white correction fluid, as was the roller of the typewriter in front of her. Dani cleared her throat.

"Hi," she bubbled.

"Hi," Dani returned. "I would appreciate it if I could have a look at an old file."

Bambi's eyebrows drew together. "What kind of file."

Dani explained that her parents had been killed, gave the date, and was pleased to discover that Bambi had a compassionate heart beneath her ample bosom. She remained standing at the counter while Bambi disappeared into an area marked File Room.

"You better be telling me the truth, Cantrell," she muttered under her breath. In her mind, she wondered how she would react if she found this portion of Tyler's story was false. He'd said the file had disappeared just after the trial.

Her heart fell when Bambi emerged carrying a thin manila folder. Dani felt an odd tightness in her chest as the woman grew closer.

"Sorry it took so long."

"No problem," Dani managed as she reached for the folder Bambi had placed on the small counter that separated them. The edges were tattered, and the file appeared to have darkened with age. The condition was consistent with her expectations, but Dani was shocked by the contents—or, more accurately, the lack thereof.

Allowing her purse to fall to the floor with a thud, she flipped open the cover and found only three documents inside.

"There must be some mistake," she told the policewoman.

"Really?" Bambi asked.

Separating the pages, Dani tapped each one with the tip of her fingernail. "There's nothing here!" she cried out. "This is a memo about the call. This is some typed statement by the patrol officer who cordoned off the house. And this," Dani said as she grabbed up the final page, "this is a copy of Stone's driver's license."

Bambi's head tilted to one side, and her expression reminded Dani of a dog trying to understand a human voice.

"Is there a problem here?"

Dani still held the grainy copy of Stone's license when she turned to face Sheriff Cassidy. "I'm astounded at the contents of this file," she told him, her tone challenging.

The round man moved toward her. Redness seemed to be creeping up from his collar, staining his cheeks. She also noted a line of moisture just above his upper lip.

"What are you doing with these?" he thundered as he ripped the paper from her hand. "Put these back where they belong!" he bellowed at the cowering officer.

"It's public record," Dani insisted.

"It's law enforcement work product," Cassidy countered.

"If that's all the work this office produced, then you didn't do a very good job."

Her assessment caused a series of veins to bulge at his temples.

"Come into my office!" he ordered before stomping down the hall.

Dani's anger began to simmer in her bloodstream as she had no alternative but to follow.

The office was cluttered and dingy. Several partially filled coffee cups ringed a massive wooden desk. When Cassidy took his seat, he motioned for her to take the one across from him.

"What exactly are you doing, Miss Baylor?"

"I was trying to review the investigation into my parents' death."

Pulling open one of the desk drawers, Cassidy removed a small tin and placed a sizable wad of tobacco between his cheek and gum. Dani found the action so distasteful that she allowed her eyes to wander to the photographs behind him on the wall. It was a collection of poorly framed pictures of the sheriff with various members of the community. Dani recognized most of the people and even found one group shot taken at the Circle B.

"What's your interest in this?"

Her mouth dropped open. "I would think that was apparent."

"It's a closed matter."

"I know that," she acknowledged. "But in light of what happened to my sister, I thought it might be worth a review of the incident."

Cassidy's knuckles whitened where he gripped the tattered arms of his chair. His small eyes narrowed, and she found his expression just short of menacing.

"Your sister? Do you have some doubts about her accident?"

I do now! her mind screamed. "Sheriff," she began, careful to rid her tone of its earlier challenge, "I just don't understand what Jennifer was doing in the trailer. Or how the fire started."

Cassidy nodded, though the veins still pulsed on either side of his ruddy face. "I'm sure we'll never know what she was doing at the trailer. I do know that the fire was electrical."

"How do you know that?" she asked.

"Fire department made a determination. I just follow what they tell me, and they said it was just an unfortunate accident."

Dani rose slowly and kept her eyes downcast. She instinctively felt that Cassidy was lying through his stained teeth. She also knew that she was wasting her time with him. She made some excuse for a hasty exit.

Hurriedly she left the building. The file was hardly a file, so Tyler must have been telling her the truth on that point. She still wasn't ready to acknowledge that he was also right about her mother. Not yet, not without some investigating of her own.

"THANKS for meeting me here," she said to David Clay as he stepped from his truck onto the charred grasses surrounding the remnants of the trailer.

"Don't mind, Miss Baylor," the lanky man drawled.

She smiled at his image where it was outlined by the last rays of daylight. "I understand you've been with the Beaumont Fire Department for seventeen years."

"Yes ma'am," he answered, almost shyly.

"And you can tell if there's been an electrical short?"

He nodded. "Usually. If there's enough evidence and it's a fairly obvious defect. If not, it would take some tests and some time."

"I'm not asking for a definitive report," she promised him. "I just want your impression."

David walked ahead of her, using a flashlight to deter the lengthening late-afternoon shadows. "How come you didn't ask the investigator for Brock's Pass to explain this to you?"

"I was afraid he might think I was questioning his report. I wouldn't want to step on any toes."

He seemed placated by her explanation. "How's Carol? I haven't seen her in a couple of months?" David asked loudly in order for her to hear his voice above the engine of a passing car. They stood with their back to the roadway.

"She's great. I've really enjoyed spending time with her."

She held the flashlight while he sifted through the ash-covered piles of wire, metal, burned fabric and other items. The stench of the fire still clung to the scene. Dani found it nearly overpowering in spots when they entered the burned shell of the trailer.

Although Dani tried to keep her feelings in check, she couldn't seem to help shivering now and again when an overwhelming sense of Jen's presence would seemingly rise from the ashes and intensify Dani's still-grieving soul. She concentrated as best she could on David's actions to try and avoid slipping in too deep a depression.

David grunted, clicked his tongue and hummed throughout the process. As night began to fall, so did her spirits. She had watched him pull and trace the wires from each outlet and switch box. Whatever he was thinking, he didn't feel the need to share. She could only assume that his silence was confirmation of the official version of the fire.

"Wasn't the wires," he announced after more than two hours of examination.

"Are you certain?"

"Not certain," he conceded. David lifted his cap and scratched the top of his head. "I don't see where they found any troubles with the wiring. I don't even know why they'd have bothered, when they saw that."

She looked at the corner of the room where David was pointing. To her it didn't look any different from the other three walls covered in dark, black soot.

"See the bubbling there?"

She moved closer. "Those blisterlike things?"

"Right," he said. "There's no way for me to know what might have caused the blisters, but if it was my investigation, I'd start there."

"What kinds of things cause blisters?"

"Accelerants."

"Gasoline? What?"

He shook his head. "I couldn't tell without lab tests."

She nodded. "But you wouldn't say this was an accident?"

David shuffled from foot to foot. "I'm not saying that. There could have been a bottle of hair spray on an end table that exploded and left those blisters. Without the proper tests, it's impossible for me to know for sure."

"But you don't think it was electrical?"

"After this brief review," he answered after a slight hesitation, "I really don't think it was wiring."

After seeing him back to his truck, she returned to the burned-out trailer. It was eerie to be there alone. The only source of light was the single beam from her flashlight and the occasional passing vehicle's headlights.

David hadn't exactly proven that there was something flawed in the investigation, but he had given her one more reason to trust Tyler. A small smile curved the corners of her lips as a vision of the handsome man danced across her brain. She was warming to the idea of having him as a confidant. His arrogance was annoying, but it also hinted at a determined streak she felt would be crucial to uncovering the truth.

"But why?" she whispered. "Why is Tyler so committed to getting to the bottom of all this? And who was the woman on the phone?"

Dani turned at the sound of a vehicle slowing down on the road. Using her hand to shade her eyes, she found herself blinded by the high beams of the car.

There was the sound of a car door opening, and she half expected to hear David's voice calling out to her. Instead, she heard the unmistakable sound of a rifle being cocked to fire.

Chapter Seven

In the split second it took her brain to decipher the sound, Dani went into action. Adrenaline pumped life into her legs as she made a dash for the wooded sanctuary behind the burned-out trailer. The first shot rang out and ricocheted off the scorched tin shell.

Using an upturned portion of the roof as a shield, Dani slipped behind it just as the bright light of a spot lamp illuminated the ash-covered space. She grunted when her knee contacted something hard. Every breath was shallow, almost painful, and she found it hard to hear above the incessant beating of her heart. The second shot pierced the metal just above her shoulder. A whooshing sound filled her ear as the bullet burned a path past her head.

Eyes wide, she scanned the area for possible alternatives. Whoever was using her for target practice had made one mistake. The beam from the light guided her through the woods abutting the remains of the trailer. Taking in a deep breath, Dani summoned her courage and ran in a zigzag pattern.

Two shots followed her into the pine forest. The first shot splintered the bark of a tree just to her left. The second was more effective. She felt the pressure before the pain. A guttural sound from deep within her throat escaped on a shocked gush of air. Her arm burned, and instinctively she lifted her hand to the wound, but continued stumbling forward into the thick underbrush. A low-hanging branch slapped at her cheek. Dani felt warm, sticky moisture begin to seep through her fingers.

"Don't think about it," she commanded herself aloud. The ground beneath her feet was rocky and uneven, making it difficult for her to maintain her speed. Another shot rang out. The bullet whizzed over her head.

Keep moving! she chanted to herself. A small noise erupted from her throat as the ground disappeared. Half tumbling, half sliding, Dani rolled down an embankment. It couldn't have taken more than a few seconds for her to reach the bottom of the ravine. When her body came to rest against a gnarled tree root, she sat perfectly still . . . waiting.

One set of footsteps caused a vibration on the earth above. It was too dark for her to see her attacker, and she prayed the opposite was also true. Slowly she eased herself against the cool ground and molded herself to a protruding root. Above her head she could see the beams of white light from the car's headlights. A long, imposing shadow spilled over the mouth of the ravine. Her heart pounded as she made out the silhouette of an armed man. He was less than twenty feet away.

Stay calm and quiet! she silently instructed herself. She wondered if the man could hear the rapid beating of her heart or the shallow, labored breaths escaping from her lips. The shadow moved closer. One booted foot tested the moss-covered ground at the top of the ridge, sending a shower of small pebbles down around her.

She was trapped. There was nothing she could do, no way she could stand and run without being seen. He cocked the rifle.

She felt around on the ground for a weapon, anything she might use to fend him off. Still, her eyes remained fixed on his slow, deliberate descent. Then she heard it . . . faint at first, then louder.

"Someone's coming!" an unidentified male voice called.

The gunman quickly retraced his steps and disappeared into the bright light. Dani listened. There was the sound of a car engine, immediately followed by the squeal of tires. She made no moves, her body paralyzed by uncertainty.

"Dani!"

Her eyes remained fixed on the top of the ravine.

"Dani!"

The light wasn't as bright as before, and the angle of the beam was different. The voice was unmistakable.

"Tyler!"

In what seemed like an instant, she felt strong arms gather her off the ground.

"Are you hurt?"

"My arm," she managed in a small voice.

"What the hell happened here?" he asked as he gently turned her in order to check her wound.

"A man shot at me."

"I know. I was near the fencing when I heard the shot. What I don't understand is why."

"I don't know," she answered.

Tyler had peeled away the tattered edges of her sleeve. His features were dark and shadowed. "It's not deep."

"Thank God," she said, gripping his forearm with trembling fingers. "Get me out of here."

Tyler helped her climb out and directed her toward the still-idling truck he'd abandoned near the trailer.

Carefully he placed her on the seat. Dani seemed unable to control the shaking of her body. By the light of the dash, she was able to see the extent of the injury to her arm. Tyler was right. There was blood, but it appeared to be little more than a deep scratch. A few inches in either direction and it probably would have been fatal.

She watched as he moved to pick up something off the ground. He still held it in his balled fist when he joined her in the cab of the truck.

"What happened?" he asked again.

Resting her head against the seat, she swallowed hard before speaking. "I met a friend of Carol's here. We discussed the fire. He left, then the mad marksman showed up."

"What'd he look like?"

Dani gave him a long look. "I only remember the gun. He had a big rifle. Other than that, I didn't see much, because of the high beams."

Tyler digested her words, then slammed his fist against the steering wheel. Opening his hand, he showed her what he had retrieved from the ground. "Teflon-coated shell."

"What does that mean?"

"It's a type of bullet with only one purpose. To kill people."

She shuddered. "Why would someone want to kill me?"

"To keep you from looking into the murder."

"My sister's or my folks'?"

"I don't think it matters."

"GOOD GRACIOUS! What happened to you?" Lupe demanded as she dropped her dish towel.

"I had a little problem out on highway 7," Dani told the concerned housekeeper.

"You're bleeding!"

"It's not as bad as it looks," Tyler said.

Dani noted the forced lightness in his tone and appreciated what he was trying to do. Lupe looked near hysteria as she shuffled toward the pantry for the first-aid kit, but Tyler's assurance seemed to have placated the woman somewhat.

"What is all the commotion?" Sandra bellowed even before she entered the kitchen. "What have you done now, Danielle? Did you wreck Jennifer's car?"

Dani managed a mirthless smile before answering, "No, Aunt Sandra."

"Then why are you covered in all that filth? Is that blood on your blouse?"

"Yes, Aunt Sandra. And no—I didn't wreck the car."

"I'll call the sheriff's department," Tyler said as he walked toward the phone.

"The sheriff? What for?" Sandra wailed.

"Someone shot at me," Dani announced. Lupe made a horrified noise. Her aunt's eyebrows drew together suspiciously.

"You must be mistaken, Danielle. I swear, you and your imag—"

"She didn't imagine this," Tyler said, interrupting her. Flattening his palm, he allowed the shiny, bronze-colored casing to roll on his outstretched hand.

It took nearly a half hour for Lupe to clean and dress her arm. Then Dani joined Tyler at the table. His eyes were clouded, and there were deep lines at the corners.

"The sheriff should be here any second," Sandra said, huffily from the doorway. "Since you insisted on inviting him out here, I've got to change."

"It's important to accessorize appropriately to report a crime," Dani said under her breath.

No sooner had her aunt left than Matt appeared. Dani could tell from the slight reddening of his cheeks that he had been keeping company with his bottle of Scotch.

"What happened?" he asked as he rushed to her side.

Dani patted the hand he placed on her shoulder and looked up into his concerned eyes. "Nothing major, Uncle Matt."

"Is that what you call getting shot at?" Tyler asked.

"Shot at?"

"I had a little run-in on highway 7," Dani told him. She filled her uncle in on the details and felt a pang of guilt when she noted the effect her words were having on him. There was a raw look in his eyes that Dani attributed to his genuine concern. "I'm fine, though. Thanks to Tyler."

Matt's head shot up, and he looked in Tyler's direction. "What were you doing out there?"

Before Tyler could answer, they were interrupted by the boisterous entrance of Sheriff Cassidy. Dani was struck by the casual way the man strolled into the kitchen, exchanging niceties with her perfectly made-up aunt.

"Well now, Miss Baylor. You had some trouble out on the highway?"

"The term *trouble* seems a bit mild under the circumstances," Dani answered. She then launched into a recital of the events. Occasionally during the retelling, Tyler would reach out and gently pat the back of her hand. Lupe appeared to be in shock, and coped by busying herself with preparing a pot of coffee. Matt looked dumbstruck, and Sandra hardly gave the fantastic story any notice.

When she finished, Cassidy turned his dull eyes on Tyler. "What were you doing out by the trailer?"

Dani saw the muscles in Tyler's jaw tense, and she could almost feel his hostility. Cassidy's accusatory tone was obviously not lost on the man.

"I was checking the fence on the east ridge."

Cassidy adjusted his belt, where it was hidden beneath his protruding belly. The movement caused the seat beneath him to creak in heavy protest. "Why were you—?"

"Sheriff," Dani cut in, "this isn't about Tyler. It was two men in a pickup."

"I thought you said you couldn't identify them."

Rolling her eyes, Dani said, "I don't know who they were, but I know they weren't Tyler."

Reluctantly, he nodded. "Have you had any run-ins with men since you've been here?"

"Except for you?" Dani returned sweetly. She saw Tyler hide his smile behind his coffee mug. His approval had the ability to lift her spirits considerably. The sheriff's neck was turning that blotchy red color. "No, Sheriff. I haven't had words with anyone since I arrived."

Cassidy struggled to his feet. His hand rested on the handle of the revolver holstered on his hip. "I'm sure it was just some boys jacklighting."

"Jacklighting?" she repeated.

"They catch an animal in their headlights and then shoot from their vehicle," Tyler explained.

"Is that legal?"

The sheriff shook his head. The movement caused one strand of thin, oily hair to fall free. "No, ma'am, but I'll be sure to look into it."

Dani gaped at the man. "That's it? You're going to treat this like some unfortunate hunting incident?"

"Oh, Danielle, please!" Sandra interjected. "The sheriff has listened to your story. What do you expect him to do?"

"Investigate?" she suggested with a pointed stare at the flabby officer. "Tyler found a bullet casing. Can't you start there?"

"The casing will only identify the gun after it's found. It can't find the gun or the shooter," Tyler said.

Cassidy, Matt and Sandra all stared at Tyler.

"He's right," Cassidy acknowledged reluctantly. "But I'll take it with me, just in case we get a break."

Tyler handed the shell over to the officer. Dani noted that the two men exchanged more than the evidence. Emotion sparkled from Tyler's rich brown eyes. His shoulders stiffened defiantly in a nonverbal challenge.

Cassidy's reaction was predictable. He glowered down at Tyler and narrowed his eyes. His mouth was nothing more than a thin, angry line. "You own a rifle, boy?"

Tyler's head turned slowly, deliberately. "Yes."

"This caliber?" Cassidy asked, using the spent shell as a prop.

"Yes."

"Sheriff," Matt said, interrupting. "Ty wouldn't shoot at Dani. You have my word."

She was grateful for the effect of her uncle's statement. Grudgingly Cassidy stepped away from the table. Dani silently thanked her uncle for his peacemaking intervention.

"I'll make out a report and have one of my officers bring it around for you to sign," he told Dani.

"That will be fine," she informed him.

"I'll see you out," Sandra offered, as if the sheriff had just dropped in for afternoon tea.

"That man's a horse's ass," Tyler grumbled as soon as Cassidy had left the kitchen.

His statement brought a sparkle of amusement to Lupe's eyes. Matt simply shrugged. He seemed to Dani to be deeply troubled. It was comforting to realize just how concerned her uncle was for her safety. She gave his hand a squeeze.

Her mind replayed Tyler's answer about the fencing. "When did we put up fencing on the east ridge?"

Tyler's eyes dropped to the ground, and she thought his shoulders tensed ever so slightly.

"We haven't actually put up the fencing. That's what I was looking at."

Dani was in a real quandary. She wanted to believe him, but something about his explanation didn't quite ring true. However, short of yelling 'liar, liar, pants on fire,' there wasn't much more she could say. And the fact that he was there had saved her life.

"I'm going to take a bath and get some sleep," she announced.

"I'll walk you up," Tyler offered.

His polite gesture inspired quite a response from her overloaded senses. As they moved toward the steps, she was keenly aware of his fluid movements. Her shoulder brushed against his solid chest, inciting a whole new array of thoughts and feelings.

When he placed his fingers at the small of her back, Dani couldn't ignore the warmth of his touch. She tried to convince herself that it was just some sort of reaction caused by her recent trauma. The clean scent she had grown to associate with him caressed her senses.

"What were you really doing out at the trailer tonight?" he asked when they reached the door to her bedroom.

Dani looked up into the full force of his eyes and felt her pulse begin to quicken. "I was looking into the cause of the fire."

One blond eyebrow arched, and his mouth curved into a lazy smile. "You wanted to know whether or not I was telling you the truth."

"That, too," she acknowledged softly.

He reached for her with one hand, allowing it to rest on her shoulder, near her collarbone. She could feel every inch of his squared fingers through the tattered fabric of her blouse. The feel of his touch wasn't nearly as powerful as the simmering passion she saw in those chocolate-colored eyes.

Dani felt her breath catch in her throat as the air between them grew palpable. It was as if a current had become engaged, filling the inches that separated them with a strong and powerful electricity. For several protracted seconds, they said nothing. Dani was too afraid of breaking the spell. She didn't know what might happen, but she didn't want to do anything that might disturb the budding bond joining them at that moment.

His eyes traveled lower, until she could almost feel him staring hard at her slightly parted lips. She knew instinctively that his thoughts were taking the same path as her own. His hand moved slowly toward her face until he cupped her cheek, his thumb resting just inches from where his eyes remained riveted.

His thumb burned a path toward her lower lip. She watched the intensity in his eyes deepen as his thumb brushed tentatively across her mouth. Gently at first, but then, with each successive movement, he applied more pressure, until Dani thought she might die from the anticipation knotting her stomach.

Raising her hand, she flattened it against his chest. She could feel his heart beating against the solid muscle. A faint moan rumbled in his throat.

His head dipped fractionally closer and she held her breath, fully expecting and wanting his kiss. His thumb continued to work its magic. The friction had produced a heat that was carried to every cell in her body. Dani swallowed.

"That first night," he began in a husky, raspy voice.

"Yes?"

"When I said I wasn't interested."

"Yes?"

"I lied."

His breath washed over her face in warm, inviting waves, but he made no move to close the gap. Gathering a handful of his shirt, Dani urged him to her. His resistance was a surprise. His thumb stilled and rested just below her lip.

His eyes met and held hers. "It would be pretty low of me to take advantage of you now."

"I wouldn't consider it taking advantage," she told him.

Careful to avoid her injury, Tyler pulled her against him, cradling her head in his hand. She could feel and hear his heartbeat.

"I would," he said.

The first stirrings of embarrassment crept into her consciousness. She felt her face grow warm with the realization that she had all but begged the man.

"Look," she said, stepping out of his arms with her head bowed. "I need a good night's sleep. Thanks for what you did tonight. I don't know how I'll ever be able to thank you enough."

"I can think of a way," he answered before he turned and walked down the hall.

Closing the door, she leaned against the cool wooden surface and fanned herself with her hand. "Close," she mumbled. "Very close."

Careful not to get the bandage wet, Dani soaked her scraped and bruised body before slipping into a satin gown. The bath did little to rid her of the euphoric flutters every time she thought about the way he had touched her. Raising her hand to her mouth, Dani closed her eyes and remembered the way his callused thumb had felt. Her attraction to Tyler was growing in leaps and bounds.

"I have to stop this," she admonished herself. Knowing full well that the only thing that might redirect her thoughts was a diversion, Dani walked over to the dresser. Nestled in the third drawer, she found the still-sealed package. Carrying it to the bed, Dani propped some pillows against the headboard and made herself comfortable.

State of Montana v. Hayden Stone. Reading the ti-tle was enough to cause a chill of foreboding to travel the full length of her spine. Taking a deep breath, Dani turned the page and began to read. The beginning was dull and dry—a bunch of promises made to the jury by the lawyers. Dani was glad to see that the case had been prosecuted by G. Franklin Meyers. As far as she knew, Mr. Meyers was still alive. She made a mental note to arrange a visit.

For the next two hours, she read through the damning testimony. Stone, who at the time of the murder had been a hand on the Circle B, had been seen fighting with her father the day before the crime was committed. Several people testified that Stone had threatened her father. The knife that was used and left in the living room by the killer was identified as belonging to Stone, and only his fingerprints were found on the weapon. The doctor testified that there were several violent stab wounds and gave the depth and a description of each one. Dani felt bile rise in her throat as she read for the first time the account of what had actually happened that night. She knew her parents had been stabbed, but until that moment, she'd had no idea that their bodies had been mutilated, as well. The doctor indicated that the knife had been thrust in, then twisted, which had resulted in deep, gouged-out injuries to both bodies.

"Good heavens." Dani gagged as she looked away from the page. There was an uncomfortable tightness in her stomach and her chest.

Everything seemed to indicate that Stone was guilty, in spite of his protestations of innocence, which had interrupted the trial time and time again. *What did you find here, Jen?*

A motion was made after the prosecution rested. The defense wanted a continuance in order to locate a material witness who could provide Stone with an alibi. The judge denied the motion. After a brief recess for lunch, the trial resumed.

That was where she discovered the first problem with the transcript. Though the page numbers were sequential, the ebb and flow of the trial seemed to take a decidedly abrupt turn. According to the typed pages, the only witness called by the defense was Stone. He sat calmly on the stand and insisted that he was being framed. He denied being at the ranch that night.

"I was at Nellie's." She read Stone's words aloud.

"Who is Nellie?" she asked as she jotted the name down on the flap of the envelope.

But the attorney didn't follow up on that line of questioning. Why? she wondered. So maybe Brock's Pass wasn't a hotbed of legal expertise; but still it didn't make sense that the attorneys would let this pass without follow-up.

Stone said that his argument with her father had been over 'the Cromwell deal.'

"What was that?" she mumbled and made another note.

Again there was no follow-up. "This is very weird," she whispered.

He said they had later made up, that the two of them had talked their differences out. He also admitted that no one had heard or witnessed the alleged resolution.

On cross-examination, Stone said he had been close with Dani's mother. "Was 'close' a thinly veiled acknowledgment that they were having an affair, I wonder?"

Stone was then asked if he knew a man named Cliff Shaw from the AAA Detective Agency.

The image of the file folder in the attic flashed across her mind. Reading on, she discovered that neither the prosecutor nor the defense followed up on that point, either. Stone admitted knowing about the detective following him, but there was nothing in the transcript to indicate why or for how long. Could Shaw be the witness the defense couldn't find? she wondered.

Thinking she might have discovered something important, Dani slipped out of bed. Wrapping her robe over her gown, she glanced at the clock before leaving her room. She hoped Tyler wouldn't mind a 2:00 a.m. visit.

The house was still, and her footsteps seemed to fill the darkness around her as she eased her way down the hall. The walk down the hall in the dark brought that old familiar lump of fear to her throat. Ever since the night of the murders, Dani had been terrified to roam around in the dark. She told herself she was being foolish, but quickened her step nonetheless.

When she reached Tyler's door, she knocked softly. No response. She knocked harder. No response. Suddenly fearful, Dani boldly pushed the door open and called out to him in a whisper. No response.

She was able to make out the bed due to the moonlight filtering through the curtains. Tyler wasn't in the room.

"Odd . . ." she whispered.

Closing the door, Dani decided to check for him in the kitchen. It, too, was deserted. She was about to give up on him when she heard the muffled sound of voices by the back door. Cautiously she moved along the wall toward the closed door. Through the curtain she was able to make out two forms. One was definitely Tyler. She could tell by the animated way he moved his hands when he spoke and the unmistakable definition of his upper body.

She took two steps closer and reached a tentative hand up to the edge of the material covering the small window. Yes, it was definitely Tyler. He had moved so that he stood facing the back door. His companion was a mystery, but unmistakably female.

Chapter Eight

"What *are* you doing?"

Startled, Dani flinched at the sound of her aunt's shrill voice. As she did so, her hand pounded against the glass portion of the door.

Sandra stood in the entryway of the kitchen, her hands planted on her hips. Her expression was stern and shriveled.

As if having Sandra glaring at her weren't bad enough, Dani soon had to contend with Tyler storming in from the rear. Pasting herself against the wall, she felt as if she were trapped on the front line, with hostile forces closing in fast from all directions.

"Danielle," Sandra began tartly, "I asked what you were doing skulking around here, in the dark, in the middle of the night."

"I...um..." she stammered under the full force of Tyler's inquisitive brown eyes.

"Yes?" Sandra prompted. "And you, Tyler? What were you doing on the back porch at this time of night?"

"Having a cigarette," he said easily.

Dani's mouth dropped open upon hearing the lie slip easily past his expertly chiseled lips.

"Do you always invite company over when you have a cigarette?" she asked him.

The flash of surprise came and went so quickly from his expression, Dani wondered if perhaps she had imagined it.

"I don't know what you're talking about," he replied. He moved past her to the cabinet next to the sink.

"Would one of you mind telling me what's going on here?" Sandra demanded.

Staring at his back, Dani realized Tyler had no intention of offering any sort of information on his clandestine meeting. Who was the woman? And why was he lying?

"I came down for some bottled water," Sandra announced. "I'm having such trouble sleeping with my back," she continued. "The piece Clayton and I are working on is that old breakfront that used to be in the living room."

"I can't believe I'm discussing furniture refinishing at two in the morning," Dani grumbled.

Sandra spun around and offered her a cold stare. "A little compassion is in order, Danielle. My restoration efforts will make this home a showplace. I know you don't care much for the history of this place, so the task falls to me."

"I'm sure it's very taxing," Dani said beneath her breath. "I'm also sure your back is as painful as my arm. You remember my arm, Aunt Sandra—where I was shot this afternoon?"

Tyler turned and smiled then, leaning against the smooth surface of the countertop.

"As usual, you're only concerned with yourself," Sandra said with a huff, waving a bottle of designer water in the air. "I'm going back to bed."

With Sandra gone, Dani eyed Tyler. "Why did you lie about the woman?"

His head tilted to one side. "I don't know what you're talking about."

Dani raised her arms and let them slap loudly against the sides of her legs. "I saw you, Tyler."

"Must have been a shadow," he said as he took a sip of water.

"Nice try," she said sarcastically. "I know what I saw."

Tyler shrugged, obviously unfazed. "What were you doing down here, anyway? Another nightmare?"

Dani shook her head. "I was looking for you."

Tyler placed the empty glass in the sink. "Now you've found me."

"I've been reading through the transcript."

"And you found something?" There was a definite excitement in his voice, and he moved toward her.

"I found something strange. Several things, in fact."

"Such as?"

"The transcript doesn't feel right," she said.

"Could you be a little more specific?"

"There's a pace that changes abruptly when the defense begins its case. It was almost like the thing had been edited."

"How could an official transcript be edited?"

"I don't know," she admitted. "But the questioning didn't flow. There's mention of a Cromwell deal, a detective named Shaw, and some woman named Nellie that Stone claimed was his alibi. The attorney never asked questions to elaborate on any of those points. I'm most curious about Cliff Shaw."

"The detective?"

"Have you talked to him?"

"Haven't been able to find him. He isn't in Brock's Pass anymore."

"What about the agency he worked for?"

"Jennifer was supposed to go check it out."

A cold sensation crawled up her spine, and Dani gave an involuntary little shiver. Was this what Jen had found in the transcripts?

He went to her side, not quite sure how to deal with the pain that clouded her wide green eyes whenever Jennifer's name came up in conversation. He reached out, resting his hand on her shoulder. She'd seen them on the porch. That was unfortunate. It wasn't the right time. Not yet. He winced inwardly, wondering how this might affect the tentative trust he'd been working so hard to foster.

"I think you need to get some rest," he said. When she lifted her face toward him, Tyler felt the familiar knot form in his gut. She looked so damned vulnerable.

"I'm not sure I know how anymore," she said with a forced smile.

He really liked her smile. "You've had a rough day."

She rolled her eyes and shook her head. "It *has* been interesting."

"Does your arm hurt?"

"Not really," she said after testing the limb. "It's a little stiff and sore, but nothing earth-shattering."

"Dani," he said softly. His hand moved from her shoulder to her face. He struggled to ignore the softness of her skin where he clutched her chin between his thumb and forefinger. He stared hard at her mouth, knowing full well it was a dangerous move. He just couldn't shake the memory of touching her. He could still feel the silky softness of her mouth, and he desperately wanted to taste her. He had spent a considerable amount of time wondering what it would be like to hold her. To kiss her.

"Yes?" she murmured.

The sound of her voice brought him back to the present. "I'll walk you up."

"Are you going to tell me about your visitor?"

Tyler gently gripped her upper arm and steered her in the direction of the stairs. "Why would I meet someone on the back porch at 2:00 a.m.?" *Why indeed?* he thought.

He was still reeling from the close call as he closed the door to his bedroom. This had all seemed so simple a few months back—quick and easy. But that had been before he knew about Dani.

He fell onto the bed, crossing his feet at the ankles. Her face flashed across his mind. How could Jennifer have been so wrong about her own sister? he wondered. Okay, so she was reserved, but he liked that. He also liked the way she seemed to cope with all the strange things that were happening.

His mouth turned down when he thought about the way she would react when she discovered the truth. When Jennifer approached him, it was supposed to be easy. She had assured him that she would take care of Danielle. Now it was up to him.

"THANKS, CAROL." Dani hung up the phone and turned to Tyler. "Shaw has a cabin near the north ridge outside of Beaumont."

"I'm impressed," he told her.

The dazzling smile he offered her caused her heart to flutter. "If we leave now, we would get there just before lunch."

"We?"

"Yes, we!" she answered. "I'm the one that wangled his current address from Carol's mother, so I'm definitely going with you."

"I don't think that's such a smart idea."

She noted the cautious expression in his eyes, but refused to be deterred. She hadn't totally forgotten about what had happened the night before—it made her uneasy just thinking about it. Tyler had definitely lied about the woman on the porch. If she stuck to him like glue, he could hardly maintain his veil of secrecy.

"You have to take me, Tyler," she told him with a devilishly superior smile. "I'm the one with the directions."

Stuffing the small rectangle of paper in her purse, Dani moved toward the door. "Coming?" she called over her shoulder.

She heard him mutter something unflattering under his breath as they stepped into the rays of the bright morning sun. The Testarossa was parked in the driveway, courtesy of the hand sent to fetch it from the trailer.

"I'll drive, you navigate," Tyler suggested as he offered her his palm.

Dani passed him the keys and went around to the passenger side. She had her fingers on the handle when the cackle sounded.

"Where are you two going?" Sandra inquired from her perch on the top step.

"To Beaumont," she answered.

"But I need help with the breakfront. I was counting on you to help me, Danielle. It's not like I ask for much."

"Sorry," she told her aunt. "Call Buck and have him send up a couple of the men."

"That's right," Sandra bellowed, "see only to your own needs!"

"She's a piece of work," Tyler observed dryly once they were safely behind the tinted glass of the car.

"That's one way of putting it." Dani shifted so that she sat angled toward him.

His strong profile was rimmed in golden beams of light. His blond hair took on rich highlights where it framed his deeply tanned face. The small space separating them held the pleasant scent of his cologne, and Dani knew her thoughts were about to wander into dangerous territory. The shirt he'd chosen was pale blue cotton. The ribbing on the sleeves outlined the well-developed biceps peeking out from the edges. His jeans were a softer blue, faded and molded to his thighs. She swallowed, hard.

"How did Carol's mother find Shaw?"

"She knows the secretary for the First Church of the Holy Redeemer. Shaw is some sort of elder, or something."

"Nice work," he said as he offered her one of those sexy half smiles.

"I've spent the last year of my life researching for my dissertation. I consider myself something of an expert."

"What's your dissertation about?"

"Varina Davis."

"Who is that?"

"Jefferson Davis's daughter. More commonly referred to as the Daughter of the Confederacy."

"How'd you get onto that?"

Dani reached up and twisted a lock of her hair. "I spent some time in Biloxi, Mississippi, and toured the Davis family home. I was fascinated by the things I saw there, so when it came time to pick a topic, I went with Varina."

"Why history?"

She thought for a second before answering. "I guess I saw *Gone With The Wind* a dozen or more times and became fascinated with the Civil War era. How about you? How did you become a private detective turned ranch foreman?"

Shaking a cigarette from the pack, Tyler flicked his lighter and inhaled until the tip glowed amber. "I worked on ranches all during school, and for a while after. I wanted a change and went to work for an insurance company. They trained me in field investigations. I decided I liked digging into other people's business."

"Like mine?"

"I'm not digging, Dani. I'm finishing a job."

"Your determination is admirable, but I don't understand why you stayed on after Jennifer..."

"I don't like things half-done."

Tyler seemed to close up after that. He offered only the occasional one-syllable response to her questions. Finally Dani gave up and busied herself by watching the varied rock formations lining the deserted strip of road. It was growing warmer by the minute. The black surface of the road glistened with ghostly images of water.

The monotony of the drive was broken only when they passed through small clusters of houses. Dani was reminded of just how desolate life in Montana could be. Odd that she didn't feel isolated, not with Tyler around.

"Is this the left?"

"Yes," she answered. "It should be about three miles up this pass."

The road was rutted and covered in a layer of brownish dust. On either side of the single lane, tall pines stood guard, offering them a haven from the hot noontime sun.

"Shaw certainly has gotten back to nature," Tyler observed when the rustic-looking cabin came into view.

The front yard was cluttered with debris, partially stripped automobiles and a full-size refrigerator. The minute Tyler stopped the car, a shaggy black dog came toward them, barking and jumping up on his hind legs.

"Think he's friendly?" she asked.

"Only one way to find out," Tyler said as he cracked the window.

Large ebony paws lurched forward, followed by the animal's snout. When Ty placed his hand near the dog's face, he was treated to a forceful series of sloppy licks.

"There's nothing quite like a boy and his dog."

"Very funny," he said as he pushed the door open. "C'mon, let's pay a visit on the apostle Cliff Shaw."

The dog greeted Dani with the same enthusiasm he had shown Tyler. "Not a very good watchdog, are you?"

The steps leading up to the house were cracked, and several nails poked up through the rotted boards. The front door wasn't in much better shape. The doorknob dangled precariously from its base, and it appeared as if a strong breeze could easily blow it in.

Tyler knocked. The dog stood between them, fanning the dust with its rapidly wagging tail.

Tyler knocked a second time.

"He must not be home," she suggested, disheartened.

Tyler went down the steps to the window. Rubbing a circle with his palm, he cupped his hands over his eyes and looked in.

"See anything?"

"Nope."

"You mean we came all this way for nothing?" she asked.

"Absolutely not," Tyler announced as he rejoined her on the steps.

"What are you doing?"

"Gaining entry."

"Isn't this illegal?" she cautioned as he pulled a long silver object from his wallet and began fiddling with the lock.

"I'm returning the man's dog."

"You don't even know if this is his dog."

"Do you live here?" he asked the dog.

It barked.

"See?"

Dani expelled a breath in the direction of her bangs. "When they arrest us, be sure to explain to the police that the dog gave you permission to break in."

"Lighten up," he said as he pushed open the door. "Hello!" he yelled into the darkened space.

"Lead the way," he told the dog.

Dani followed behind them, her eyes wide as she tried to make sense out of the shadows.

"Ouch!"

"What?" she asked. For some reason, she was whispering like a criminal.

"I hit my shin."

"On what?"

"If I knew that, I wouldn't have run into it."

"Don't get testy," she told him. Reaching behind her, Dani found the doorjamb. Feeling the wall to the left, she found the switch and gave it a flick. Light from a large table lamp spilled into the dingy interior.

There was only one room. There was a kitchen area, complete with soiled dishes and a full complement of preprepared dried foods; a living area cluttered with newspapers and piles of junk mail; and another area she assumed was a bedroom. There was a mattress—no box spring—covered with a worn and faded sheet. The wad of fabric at the foot of the bed appeared to be a makeshift blanket, but Dani wasn't going anywhere near it.

"This place is disgusting."

"Yep," Tyler agreed as he moved about the room. "I don't think Cliff will win any awards for decorating excellence."

"Look at this," she called out. Tyler instantly appeared at her side. "Look at the return address."

"Brock's Pass Sheriff's Department," Tyler read. He picked the envelope up off the table and eased apart the edges. "Nothing."

"Yes, but why is this Cliff Shaw getting mail from Cassidy?"

"We could ask the dog," Tyler suggested with a wry smile. The dog trotted over, tongue dangling and tail wagging.

Dani reached down and patted his head. "What about that pile?" She pointed toward a stack of loosely stacked file folders. Following Tyler, they crossed the scuffed and creaking floor.

"This could be something," he said as he tugged his pant legs and squatted in front of the disarray.

"This could take hours!" Dani groaned. "There must be a hundred folders here."

"One hundred sixteen."

Dani twirled at the sound of the voice coming from the doorway. A white-haired man brandishing a shotgun stared back at her. The dog trotted over and stood next to his master.

Chapter Nine

"Tyler?" She said his name in a high-pitched voice.

"No need for the gun, pal," he said as he stepped in front of her.

Dani placed one hand on his back and peeked around him. The white-haired man still held the barrel level, at about the same height as Tyler's chest.

"Depends on your point of view, son," he responded in a gravelly voice.

"We knocked," Tyler began.

"And the door just fell open?"

"Martha Spangler sent us," Dani announced. Her explanation caught the older man's attention. He eyed her curiously from behind the gun. "She gave me your address."

"Why would you be needing my address?"

"I'm Danielle Baylor," she began.

"Milton's girl?"

"Yes, sir," she answered quickly. "I'm looking into my parents' murder, and your name came up. You are Cliff Shaw, aren't you? From the AAA Detective Agency?"

He nodded and slowly lowered the gun so that it rested in the crook of his arm. "I've been expecting someone to come around."

"Why is that?" Dani asked as she stepped around Tyler.

"Got a letter from ol' Bubba."

"Why would Sheriff Cassidy write to you?" Tyler asked.

Cliff sauntered into the room, favoring his right leg. "Have a seat, Miss Baylor. I'm not young enough to stand around talking no more. Gotta do most things from my chair."

"Thank you," she managed.

After the man sat down and propped the gun in the corner next to him, the dog rested his head in Shaw's lap. Tyler was behind her, his hand on her shoulder.

"You were going to tell me why Cassidy sent you a letter?" Dani said.

Shaw nodded. "I can't believe that old fool is still sheriff."

"That makes two of us."

"He wanted to make sure I remembered what he'd done for me," Shaw continued.

"What was that?"

Shaw smiled then, deep crevasses forming on either side of his dull blue eyes. "I got into a bit of a scrape a few years back. Cassidy fixed it so I didn't get no jail time."

"Is that what he wrote to you about? Your problem with the law?"

"No, ma'am." Shaw chuckled. "He wanted to make sure I was keeping to myself."

"Keeping what to yourself?"

"My investigation of Stone."

Dani swallowed. "You investigated the murder?"

"No, no," Shaw said with a fervent shake of his head.

"I thought you said—"

"I was investigating Stone before the murders."

"Then why does Cassidy want you to keep quiet?"

"'Cause I never believed Stone did it, and Cassidy knows it."

"Forgive me, Mr. Shaw," Dani began. "I'm not following you. If your investigation didn't have anything to do with the murder, why does Cassidy care if you tell people about it?"

"It might cause some folks to ask questions Cassidy don't want asked."

"Were my mother and Stone having an affair?"

A fraction of a second passed before Shaw nodded. "Yes, ma'am. But it was over before the killings."

"Then why were you investigating Stone?" she asked.

"I was hired to make sure the affair had really ended."

"Who hired you?"

"Nellie."

"Nellie!" Dani wailed excitedly.

Shaw nodded and said, "She was Stone's girlfriend."

His explanation was interrupted by a sudden eruption of barking from the dog. The animal loped toward the door, yelping and dancing on his hind legs.

Tyler squeezed her shoulder as Shaw rose in response to a loud knock at the door.

"Afternoon, Cliff," Clayton Brightwood drawled. The newcomer's expression stilled when his eyes traveled to Dani's face. "Danielle," he added.

"What brings you out here?" Shaw asked.

"Same old thing," Clayton answered. Removing his hat, he entered the room.

Shaw turned to them and said, "Clayton's been trying to buy my land out from under me for the better part of three years now."

"That's right," Clayton said with a smile. "Gonna get it, too." He walked to the table, but made no move to sit. "What about you folks? What brings you out this way?"

"We were just visiting," Tyler answered.

Dani felt a slight tug on her shoulder.

"But we've got to be going," he added.

"What?" she all but screamed.

"It's a long trip back to the ranch, and we've already taken enough of Mr. Shaw's time."

"But we—"

"Let's go, Dani," he said forcefully.

Grudgingly she allowed Tyler to escort her from the dilapidated cabin. Her ire was almost as intense as the afternoon sun.

"What did you do that for?" she demanded as soon as they reached the car. "You didn't give him a chance to tell us about Nellie or about Cromwell."

He didn't respond until after he'd started the car and shifted into Reverse. "I didn't think it was such a good idea to continue once Brightwood got there."

Shaking her head, Dani turned in the seat and regarded his stiff profile. "We could have waited until
Mr. Brightwood left."

He shrugged and shook a cigarette out of the pack.
Dani watched with wide eyes as he rolled the filter
around on his tongue.

"Don't you think it's just a bit too coincidental that
Brightwood would suddenly put in an appearance? All
the way out here?"

Her head fell to one side. "Clayton is always buying up land. He probably owns most of the county by
now."

"So what does a rancher want or need with a hunk
of mountain?"

Suspicion crept slowly up her spine. "You think
Clayton showed up because we were there?"

"It's a definite possibility."

WITH TYLER tending to his responsibilities at the
ranch, Dani set out for some investigating of her own.
Her first stop was the home of G. Franklin Meyers.
She drove through the business district of Brock's Pass
before turning down one of the tree-lined side streets.

The former prosecutor practiced law from the
ground floor of his family's Victorian home. She
parked in front and glanced briefly at her reflection
before gathering her handbag and marching toward
the door. She sucked in her breath after climbing the
steps, and knocked rapidly against the aged, wooden
door.

"Yes?"

His shock of thick white hair was neatly combed around his weathered face. He wore the standard uniform of the area—jeans and a Western-cut shirt. The only hint of his prosperity was the bright red snakeskin boots screaming out from beneath his pant legs.

"Mr. Meyers, I'm Danielle Baylor. I'd like a few minutes of your time."

His bushy eyebrows arched upward as he stepped to one side of the polished door.

The interior of the house was refreshingly cool and surprisingly feminine. Everywhere she looked she spotted doilies. It appeared as though a giant snowstorm had been visited upon the arms of every chair, sofa and tabletop.

"Have a seat," he said pleasantly, pointing to a yellow velvet sofa off to one side.

"Thank you." She smiled as she perched herself on the edge of the plump cushion. "I'd like to talk to you about the Stone case."

His mouth pulled into a tight line, but he nodded as he took the seat across from her. "Unfortunate incident."

"Yes," she agreed, thinking the description a bit mild, considering the outcome.

"I was sorry to hear about your sister," he said. "She was here to see me about six months back."

"Really?"

"Uh-huh. She wanted to talk to me about the Stone matter. Same as you."

"What sort of information was she after?"

Meyers rubbed his chin. "She wanted to know what I remembered. My impressions at the time of the trial."

"And?" she prompted.

He waited to speak until a clock finished chiming the hour. "Stone killed your parents."

He said it with such surety and finality.

"What about the inconsistencies?"

"You mean the alibi witness?"

Dani nodded.

"I don't think there was a word of truth to it. If he'd have been with that woman, as he'd claimed, she would have come forward."

"What can you tell me about her? Nellie, wasn't it?"

"I know she was young. Poor, like Stone. I think they had a child together. Jonathan, that was his name. But Stone never married her. I'm sure that's why she never came forward. Marital privilege wouldn't have applied, and she'd have been forced to tell the truth, or face jail time if she lied."

"Do you recall her last name?"

"Not offhand. Seems to me that nobody ever called her anything other than Nellie."

Dani felt her enthusiasm begin to falter. "What about the detective?"

"Shaw," Meyers supplied with a derisive little laugh. "The defense couldn't put him on the stand. At the time of the trial, he was under investigation for breaking and entering. He had this bad habit of hiding in closets and taking pictures. If it hadn't been for Cassidy, I think Shaw would have done time."

"Can you tell me about the Cromwell deal? Wasn't that what Stone and my father were supposed to have argued over before the murder?"

Myers's wan smile brought a certain sadness to his wise blue eyes. "Cromwell Realty came into Brock's Pass with delusions of turning this place into a ski resort. Kinda like Aspen, I guess. Anyway, twenty-plus years ago they caused quite a stir with their visions of tourists and grand hotels."

"Stone opposed the development?"

"Most did," Meyers said easily. "Your father, too. Milt thought the Cromwell people were pretty slick and shady."

"If they shared the same views on the subject, what were my father and Stone fighting about the day before he died?"

"Stone claimed that he had information that your father was going to sell out."

"Why did he think that?"

"No one knew."

Dani's shoulders slumped forward. "Do you know where I might be able to find Nellie?"

He looked up toward the crown molding, his face crumpled in concentration. "I don't remember just now. I haven't really thought of her for nearly twenty years. When she sat in court, I half expected her to testify."

"She was in court?"

"Sure. Sat through the trial every day."

"Why didn't you call her to the stand to refute the defense's implication that he had an alibi? Wasn't that kind of risky?"

His eyebrows drew together, and his mouth turned down in an obvious frown. "I did call her to the stand. She refused to say a word, and the judge found her in contempt."

"Why isn't that in the transcript?" she asked.

"It is," Meyers stated simply.

"Not the copy I read."

"There must have been some clerical error," Meyers suggested with a shrug.

"But the pages were numbered correctly," she insisted.

"Look," Meyers said as he got to his feet, "maybe you should make another request for the transcript. I'm sure it was nothing other than some county employee not being real careful."

Having risen, Myers had obviously said all he was going to say on the subject. Dani took the hint and, rising herself, she followed him to the door and thanked him for his time.

It wasn't the most productive encounter she'd ever had, but she felt she was closing in on some of the secrets.

The sun lingered just above a band of menacing clouds coming over the horizon, forcing Dani to abandon her investigation for the day. She wasn't about to be out on the highway after dark, in bad weather, not when someone had gone to such great pains to show her the dangers. She shivered as she recalled the harrowing incident at the trailer.

Turning the car around in the street, she headed back through town. She was stopped at the only light when her attention was drawn to two figures engrossed in animated conversation in front of the luncheonette.

"What in the world?" she whispered.

Her words were lost on a sudden, violent wind that rattled the car. The light overhead swayed as litter swirled in the street.

Tyler reached one hand up to save his Stetson and, as he did so, his eyes met hers. His expression clouded before he motioned to her.

She eased the car off to the side of the road, but kept her eyes fixed on the baffling scene. Grabbing her purse, she dashed across the street.

"What are you doing in town?" he asked without preamble.

"Nice to see you too, Tyler," she returned. Her eyes immediately went to the second man.

"Hello, Dani," he mumbled against another gust of wind.

"Sam," she said, acknowledging him frigidly.

"You didn't answer my question," Tyler stated.

"I don't recall any laws being passed that require me to inform you of my every move," she told him.

"I've been looking for you for the past hour."

"Why?"

"Tell her, Sam," Tyler instructed.

Sam shuffled his feet under the intensity of her stare. "I just mentioned to Ty that I was at your place this morning."

She looked from man to man. "And?"

"We were helping your aunt with the breakfront when she told my father that you two had gone off to

Beaumont after you got a phone call about some man named Shaw.''

"Keep going," Tyler told Sam.

"When I told Dad, he took off. He was gone most of the afternoon."

Her eyes met Tyler's. "You think that's how he knew we were at Shaw's?"

He nodded. "Apparently your aunt clued him in on your call to Carol's mom."

"Why would Aunt Sandra be discussing my activities with your father?" she asked Sam.

"I don't know," he answered quickly. "But the two of them are real . . . close."

"Why don't we go and have a talk with my aunt?" Dani suggested.

"Can't," Sam interjected. When she gave him a questioning look, he added, "Power lines are down on the highway. I don't think you'll be able to get back to the ranch before morning."

"I STILL DON'T THINK this is such a hot idea," she grumbled as she followed Tyler toward the massive staircase that dominated the lobby.

Another fierce-sounding crash of thunder rumbled through the small hotel.

"Would you rather be out in that?"

"I suppose not," she was forced to admit.

"It could be worse," he said with a wink. "I could have taken Sam up on his offer to put us up at his place for the night."

"Not hardly," she said with a scoff as she watched him insert a key into the door.

The room was cozy. Nothing fancy, just a bed, a nightstand, two chairs and a small table. The Parker Hotel did very little business. The rooms were usually home to the occasional salesman or wandering environmentalist.

A flash of lightning supplemented the light from the overhead fixture. Dani knew the churning in the pit of her stomach wasn't from the storm holding them prisoner. It was from the realization that she was alone, in a hotel room, with a dangerously attractive man.

"Is something wrong?" he asked.

"No," she answered, trying to force a lightness into her tone. "I'm just fine."

He moved toward her then, tossing his hat on the bed on the way. "Want me to order something from the kitchen?"

She laughed nervously. "There is no kitchen."

His eyebrows drew together. "Then how about if I make a run to Mary's? You must be hungry. It's almost nine."

"You don't have to go out in this weather," she insisted.

"What about dinner?"

She shrugged and took a step backward. Food didn't seem terribly important at the moment. Not when all her senses were focused on the way his rain-dampened shirt hugged his impressive torso.

"I'm not hungry," she told him.

"I am," he told her, in a low, unnervingly sensual voice.

He came closer, virtually trapping her between the door and the massive expanse of his chest.

"Relax, Dani," he said.

The warmth of his breath caressed her upturned face. Dani searched his eyes. She found a surprising softness in their inky black depths. The gentleness, coupled with unmistakable desire, began to immediately chip away at her reservations. The air between them crackled with as much intensity as the storm raging outside.

"I don't think I can relax," she admitted.

His head tilted to one side and he gave her that sexy half smile that did nothing to defuse the situation. His hands moved and came to rest against the wall on either side of her head. He leaned into her, his taut body just slightly pressing against hers.

"Tyler?"

"Yes?"

She took in a breath, hoping to muster her quickly crumbling composure. Would it really be so bad to let him hold her? No, her mind answered. So long as she didn't let it go too far.

"What are you doing?"

"I'm trying to seduce you," he said without hesitation.

"Why?"

His smile widened. "Probably for all the usual reasons."

"Isn't this a little sudden?"

"No," he said as he brushed his lips against her forehead.

"Well," she said as she turned her head slightly, "it is for me."

Easing back somewhat, he looked down at her. "If this is about your experience with Sam, I'll back off."

She shook her head. "This has nothing to do with Sam. I'm not some permanently scarred emotional cripple."

"Good," he murmured as he placed another kiss against her temple.

"But that doesn't mean I'm ready to jump into bed with you."

"Who said anything about jumping into bed?" His lips grazed her other temple.

"Isn't that what usually happens as a result of this?"

A chuckle formed deep within his throat, and he rested his forehead against hers. "I like to think of it as getting to know one another. Sex and seduction are two different things."

Her blood pressure spiked at the remark. "I just thought . . ."

"I'm not asking you to think, Dani," he said as one squared finger wandered down around the curve of her cheekbone. "I'm not asking you for anything you aren't willing to give, either."

There was such sincerity in his voice. Such passion in those eyes. Her skin burned where he touched her. She marveled at the feel of his body against hers, the scent of soap and tobacco caressing her senses. It was hard to resist. And Dani wasn't all that sure that resistance was what she wanted.

Tentatively, she reached for him. It was like touching fire. He was so solid. She was fighting the pleasure of being so close to him. It was decision time. Mentally, she silenced that annoying voice of reason, and allowed only the promise of immense pleasure to rule her actions.

She was soft, pliant, and he felt as if he'd explode from the sweet torture of being near her. He was teetering on the brink of his control, battling to keep himself in check. It was a monumental task. The scent of fresh flowers clung to each silky strand of hair he pulled through his fingers. Her skin was even softer, and tinged with a faint blush of desire. She was breathtaking. He took in her features one by one. Admiring the deep green of her half-closed eyes. Admiring the feathery lashes that fluttered each time his hands touched her face. Admiring her perfectly sculptured lips.

"You're beautiful," he told her, just as his mouth found hers. His thumbs probed the sensitive spot on her throat just below her ears. He felt the soft moan, though no sound penetrated the cultivation of his kiss.

Her lips were soft and warm beneath his. Slowly he began his exploration of her mouth. She tasted like heaven—sweet and powerful—but his thoughts were definitely moving toward sin. He tilted her head back and savored everything.

Reluctantly he pulled back, just far enough to take in the sight of her passion-glazed eyes and her slightly parted lips. Her breathing was as quick and shallow as his own.

"I think you're incredible," he whispered.

Tyler positioned his mouth just above hers. He waited only a second before he felt her push toward him. He needed no more encouragement.

It was the passion that had caught him unawares. He'd expected restraint, possibly even shyness. What he felt was wave after wave of fierce, fiery ardor that seemed to consume them both. Her hands flattened against his chest as he held her tightly to him. He could feel the soft tracing of her fingernails as his tongue invaded the recesses of her mouth.

Holding her—kissing her—was like a euphoria he had only imagined. Dani was soft and sensual beneath his hands. Giving in to his desire, his fingers contacted the hollow of her throat. Tyler deepened his kiss. Somehow he felt as if he would die from pure ecstasy. Her skin was like warm velvet. He stroked the outline of her collarbone and was delighted when Dani responded by arching herself against his now-rigid body. While his one hand continued its investigation of her, his other wound around to capture her small waist. He could feel each vertebra of her spine as he angled her slightly to one side.

His fingers worked their way to the top button of her shirt, wavering just a second before deftly undoing the barrier. Releasing her mouth, Tyler's eyes moved to where pale ivory lace outlined the rise of her creamy breast. Her breathing was as ragged and uneven as his own. Slowly and ever so gently, Tyler slipped one finger beneath the feminine wisp of material, playfully teasing his way inside her teddy.

Dani made a small sound as his fingers brushed the taut nipple. He felt her hands begin to massage the muscles of his chest, causing an exciting friction with the mat of hair and cloth covering him.

Reluctantly he tore his eyes from the faint contour of her breast and looked up to find her eyes glazed, but still guarded. The pulse at her throat raced in time with his own. Lowering his head, Tyler tasted the skin at her throat, kissing his way lower. Dani responded by pressing herself against him with renewed enthusiasm, until Tyler could feel every inch of her supple body. It was his turn to moan.

Lifting her, he held her off the ground as his mouth moved to nuzzle the valley between her breasts. Her skin was heated, glowing with a thin sheen of perspiration. His hand reached for and found the next button of her blouse. Passion clouded his dexterity, and suddenly Tyler was no longer interested in patience. Gripping the side of her shirt, he tugged, none too gently, until he heard the tinkling sound of the buttons as they scattered around his feet. Cupping her breast in his hand, he forced his way through the lace. His mouth closed hungrily over the tawny peak.

"God, Dani..." he whispered against her skin.

Tyler felt her reach out and capture his head between her hands in response to his words. Her gentle urging nearly sent him over the edge. Somewhere in the deep recesses of his mind, Tyler knew he should slow down. Probably even stop. He wasn't really interested in the recesses of his mind. Not when he had his own personal slice of heaven.

"Tyler!" She called his name urgently. "Tyler!" she said, more forcefully.

His head lifted away from her, allowing cool air to replace the heat of his mouth.

She held his head between her hands as her brain warred with her body. He looked up at her with unbridled passion in his eyes.

For a brief time, no words passed between them. Tyler finally broke the silence.

"I'm sorry about your blouse."

Dani, feeling instantly self-conscious, allowed her fingers to move to the edges of the torn fabric as she covered herself. The heat was still there—that all-consuming fire that had very nearly robbed her of her ability to control herself. Ducking under his arm, she moved to the opposite side of the room. Suddenly she was unable to meet his eyes.

"I'm sorry—"

"Shh," he murmured, interrupting her. "I'm the one who should apologize. I don't know what came over me."

"I have an idea," she quipped, but kept her face turned toward the rain-spattered window.

"I'll get a needle and thread from the front desk," he offered. She could hear him collecting the buttons from the floor.

"This shouldn't have happened."

"You're wrong," he said as he came up behind her. He was so close, Dani could almost feel the outline of his body. "It happened because we're attracted to each other."

"But we're old enough to keep from acting on our attraction," she argued.

"No," he said, spinning her to face him. "We're old enough to act on our feelings responsibly."

Feelings! Did he mean emotional, or just physical? she wondered silently. If his expression was any indication, Tyler wasn't treating what had happened like some casual encounter. His face was tensed, as if he, too, were struggling with the same conflicting thoughts that were just beginning to surface.

"We hardly know each other," she said, then blushed at how ridiculous her words sounded. She could hardly tell him that what she was beginning to feel was more than lust—and that it frightened her.

He smiled. "I know I enjoy being with you."

"Is that why we're constantly rubbing each other the wrong way?"

"Personally, I liked the way you were rubbing me a minute ago."

Dani slapped his upper arm and felt her face flame. "I didn't mean that literally."

"Pity," he said, with a wicked wink as punctuation. His expression stilled and grew serious. His eyes searched her face. "I am attracted to you, Dani. Believe me, I didn't expect this to happen."

Was that regret in his tone? "Neither did I."

"No," he amended, "I mean, I didn't expect to meet someone like you. I'm just finding out there's a lot more to you than Jennifer let on."

"Meaning?"

"I was expecting someone more stiff. More prissy."

"Prissy?"

"Jennifer kind of hinted that your problems with Sam had left you—"

"Look," she told him, "I didn't have the problem. Sam did."

"Have you ever considered the situation from his point of view?"

"I—I don't believe this!" she stammered. "He doesn't have a point of view. I said no, and he didn't listen."

"He didn't rape you, either."

"He would have, if I hadn't screamed loud enough to wake every man in the bunkhouse."

"All I'm saying is that the guy made a mistake in judgment when he was seventeen. You might want to consider lightening up on him."

"Why should I do that?"

Tyler moved forward and placed his hand on her cheek. "Because it's the right thing to do."

"No," she countered stiffly. "He was the one who should have done the right thing."

"What if he didn't know the difference?"

Dani felt her mouth drop open. "How can you not know the difference?"

"He learned his manners from his father. From what I know of Clayton, he isn't exactly a perfect role model."

He was looking at her with kindness and compassion in his rich brown eyes. It riled her to think he had the ability to make her feel guilty about what had happened after all these years. Okay, so maybe it was a long time ago. And maybe there was something to be said for his argument about Clayton's influence. But she wasn't quite willing to absolve Sam. Not yet.

DANI AWAKENED before dawn with a plan already forming in her head. Tyler had gotten her a needle and thread, as promised, and she made quick work of fixing her blouse. The hotel was still and quiet as she crept from her room. If her plan worked, she would treat Tyler to lunch and their first real lead. She thought about waking him, but preferred the idea of surprising him.

There were puddles all along the sidewalk, thanks to the torrential rains of the night before. But this day promised to be clear and sunny. With any luck, the road crews could clear the power lines in no time. "I certainly didn't miss Aunt Sandra," she acknowledged as she walked toward the newspaper office.

"Good heavens! What are you doing out and about this time of day?"

"Hi, Mr. Grimes," she said. "I'm glad to see you're still a morning person."

"Sets a good example for the delivery boys," he answered.

Though she guessed him to be in the vicinity of eighty, Mr. Grimes was still the editor-in-chief of the *Brock's Pass Chronicle*.

"Do you keep birth announcements on file?"

He nodded. "Clear back to World War II."

Dani explained that she was looking for an announcement for a Jonathan Stone, and spent the next two hours in a futile search of an antiquated index.

"It's not here," she finally admitted.

"And you don't know the mother's name?"

"Only her first name."

"Have you tried the courthouse?"

Dani smiled at the elderly man and dashed out the door. The courthouse was just a few blocks away. She debated calling Tyler. She'd left the hotel without leaving a note or anything, thinking she'd be back long before he even noticed. It was now nearly ten, and she suspected he'd be miffed by her disappearance.

"You'll forgive me when I find Jonathan Stone," she mumbled as she entered the building.

Her first stop was the criminal desk. A middle-aged woman reluctantly walked up to the counter and asked if she could help.

"I received an incomplete copy of a trial transcript." Dani reached into her bag and produced a tattered receipt, which she passed to the woman.

The woman's expression stilled, and Dani noted that a few beads of perspiration popped out on the thin film of hair above her upper lip. She wiped at the moisture with her left hand. Dani could have sworn the woman's fingers trembled slightly.

"I'll have another one made. It'll take three business days," she said without ever looking up.

Dani nodded as she quietly studied the clerk. Was it her imagination, or did the woman look nervous?

"Is there some problem?" she asked.

The woman's eyes remained fixed on the form she'd been completing.

"No."

"Are you sure?"

"Yes," she said as she shoved the triplicate order form at Dani. "Sign here."

If Dani had any inclination to press the woman, she made it impossible by turning on her crepe soles and disappearing between large columns of folders.

Vital records were housed in the basement, and Dani was given instructions by a deputy positioned by the front entrance. The county's record-keeping system was far superior to that of Mr. Grimes. In no time at all she was handed a huge ledger with several cross-references.

"Where are you, Jonathan?" she said when she had the book.

He was on the third page—fifth entry. Stone, Jonathan Tyler. Father: Hayden Stone. Mother: Nellie Cantrell.

Chapter Ten

"Get away from my car!"

"Dani?" he said cautiously as he moved away from the hood of the Testarossa.

He quickly moved so that his large body prevented her from opening the door. Steeling herself, she looked toward the sky and fought to keep her tears in check.

"What's wrong?"

"Get away from me, Tyler."

His hand reached out and cupped her chin. She glared up at him. His expression was one of shocked curiosity.

"What's gotten into you?"

Shrugging away from his touch, she squared her shoulders and cleared her throat. "You're a liar, Cantrell. The charade is over! I know!"

It was apparent from the slight widening of his eyes that he realized she had found him out. She could almost hear the deceitful wheels turning inside his head.

"I mean it, Tyler. Get out of my way."

"It isn't what you think," he began softly.

"Oh, really?" she returned hotly. "You lied to me from the word *go*. I don't know what your motivation is, but I'm sure it has less to do with me and everything to do with your father."

"Let me explain," he said as his hand tentatively went to her shoulder.

Dani brushed it away. "Do not touch me!" she said through clenched teeth.

She heard his deep intake of breath, but she wasn't about to fall for the pained expression marring his handsome face. Not this time. Not anymore.

"Give me five minutes, Dani. Please?"

"Why should I?" she countered.

"Please?"

She lowered her eyes, wondering why she was even considering his request.

"Please?" he said again.

There was an urgent, almost pleading quality to his deep voice, and Dani hated the fact that he was actually beginning to get to her. Confusion mingled with the hurt and disappointment that had her on the verge of tears. She silently vowed she would not cry. Not yet.

"Five minutes," she told him grudgingly.

Tyler wasted no time. Grasping her hand, he pulled her toward the park. Finding a bench, he tugged her down next to him.

"I am Hayden Stone's son."

"A fact you should have mentioned to my family before you fraudulently inserted yourself into—"

"Jennifer knew."

Her eyes met his. She regarded him warily. "What do you mean?"

"That's why she hired me."

"How did Jennifer know about you? Yesterday was the first I ever heard that Stone had a son."

"Jennifer knew my mother. That's how she found me."

"The woman on the porch," Dani surmised.

"Was my mother."

Using slightly trembling fingers, Dani raked through her hair. "Why didn't you tell me?"

"I didn't know how you'd react," he answered.

Shaking her head, Dani simply gaped at the tall man. "How am I supposed to react?"

"I thought about telling you last night," Tyler continued.

"Was that before or after you tried to get me into bed?"

His eyes darkened and narrowed. "The two aren't related. Last night was as much a surprise to me as it was to you."

"You lied about my sister. You lied about who you are. Am I just supposed to believe you now because you say so?"

"No, but I'd like a chance to prove to you that I'm being up-front with you."

"And how do you propose to do that? Call in a psychic, so I can talk to Jen in the great beyond?"

"I was thinking of something a bit more conventional."

THERE WAS NOTHING to break the monotony of the silence. Dani was too absorbed in her thoughts to pay much attention to their destination. *How could I have been so stupid?* she groaned inwardly. And why am I so attracted to a man who does nothing but lie to me? A man who turns out to be the son of the man who killed my parents, no less.

"Where are we?" she asked when he stopped in front of a modest modular home planted in the center of some overgrown field.

"I thought you might like to meet my mother."

Dani's eyes grew wide as he helped her from the car.

They had reached the porch when the screen door screeched open. Dani's heartbeat increased as she watched the small woman emerge.

Nellie Cantrell was a tiny thing, with heavy shoulders that seemed to drop forward in surrender. Dani noted just a hint of what must have been youthful beauty. Her oval face was drawn, the skin wrinkled and leathery. But there was no mistaking her connection to the broad-shouldered man next to her. Nellie had the same rich brown eyes, though hers were clouded with a pitiful sadness.

She stared at Dani briefly before turning her attention to her son. There seemed to be some softening of her weary features when she tilted her head back in order to offer him a small smile.

Tyler stepped up and placed a light kiss on her cheek. Watching the scene, Dani felt a plethora of emotions churning in her stomach. Intellectually, she knew that neither Tyler nor his mother was responsible for Hayden's heinous crimes. Still, she felt as if she were being unfaithful to her parents' memory just by being here.

"I'm Nellie," the woman said after Tyler had whispered something into her ear.

She didn't extend a hand to Dani. She just patted at one of the graying strands of hair matted against her forehead.

"Come on in," Tyler suggested when Dani remained mired to the bottom step.

The interior was as bland and nondescript as the exterior. The furniture was a mismatched collection of diverse motifs. It was neat and clean and decorated with photographs and inexpensive souvenirs.

"Have a seat," Nellie suggested, wiping her hands on the sides of her jeans.

Dani mumbled a courtesy and stiffly sat in a reupholstered recliner. A breeze wafted through the living room, bringing with it the scent of sweet flowers and the unrelenting humidity.

Nellie sat across from her. Dani guessed that the woman's tentative stare probably mirrored her own. Silently she wondered if Nellie was as nervous as she.

"We need to fill Dani in," Tyler began.

"You should have filled me in from the beginning," she said.

He had the good sense to actually look repentant. He sat next to his mother, his large, squared fingers laced over one knee.

"She knows?" Nellie asked, though she appeared to relax a bit.

"She doesn't believe me anymore, so I thought it would be a good idea to bring her by here," Tyler explained.

"Given your affinity for lying to me, it only stands to reason that I would be leery of anything you said."

Nellie smiled then, without the sadness. "Please don't blame Ty," she said. "I only agreed to help Jennifer on the understanding that I would be kept out of it."

"Help Jennifer what?" Dani asked.

Nellie rose, walked into the kitchen and pulled bottles of soda from the refrigerator. As she popped the metal tops, she said, "Your sister came to me several months ago. I was sorry to hear what happened."

"Thank you."

Dani watched as Nellie carried the bottles in. A thin layer of condensation dampened her hand as she accepted the drink. Nellie paused long enough to take a long pull from the bottle.

"Why did Jennifer come to see you, Mrs. Cantrell?"

"It's Miss," she said. "She told me she had overheard some things that had made her suspicious about the verdict."

"What sort of things?"

"She didn't say, exactly. She found out I didn't testify, and she wanted to know why." Nellie's brown eyes glazed over.

"Why didn't you?" Dani asked.

Tyler's only reaction to her question was a slight tensing of the muscles near his jawline. In spite of his obvious strong feelings, he reached over as she watched and patted his mother on her slumped shoulder.

"It was a long time ago, Miss Baylor. Things was real different then."

"But if you had information that could have impacted the verdict, you should have come forward."

Her words inspired the ire of the other woman. "That's easy for you to say. You wasn't the one with a boy to feed and clothe. I wasn't about to see Ty go off to some state home."

"Wait," Dani said, waving her hand in the tension-thick air. "I was not trying to offend you, Miss Cantrell. If it sounded that way, I apologize. I'm just trying to understand the sequence of events."

"Let me," Tyler told his mother. "Twenty years ago, my mother did come forward. She told the defense attorney that my father was with her on the night of the murder."

"Then why didn't you testify?"

"'Cause of the sheriff," Nellie answered dully.

"Sheriff Cassidy?"

Nellie nodded. "When he interviewed me, I told him exactly what happened. Hayden was with me. We had dinner together. Some time later, after the rains, he went out. Said he had to see your daddy."

"So Stone wasn't actually with you all night?"

Nellie wrung her hands. "'Cept for about an hour and a half, we was together."

"The hour and a half during which my parents were killed?"

"Uh-huh," Nellie answered.

"Then you didn't testify because you knew Stone had gone to my house that night to have it out with my father?"

Nellie's laugh was low and guttural. "He wasn't going to have it out with nobody. Hayden was so scared your daddy would find out about him and your mama that all he wanted was to make peace."

Dani took in a deep breath. "Hayden and my mother were having an affair. He was at my house, alone, on the night it happened. And there is still some question in your mind about his guilt?"

Tyler rose and came to her side. "My father saw the murder, Dani. He didn't commit it."

"Hayden was a cheat," Nellie added, "but he wasn't no killer."

"He saw the killer, but didn't say anything at his trial?" Dani asked.

"No," Tyler answered.

He reached over and placed one finger under her chin, forcing her to meet his intense eyes.

"He was outside the house. He watched from the window."

Dani was having a hard time digesting everything. She felt bombarded by conflicting thoughts, emotions and images. Her brain was working at a fever pitch just to follow the fragmented conversation.

"So why wasn't any of this brought out at the trial?" she managed to ask in a small voice.

"He didn't see the murderer," Tyler explained.

"But surely he saw something that would have proved his innocence. Something his attorney could have used."

"Cassidy made sure that didn't happen," Nellie said, with obvious disdain.

"How did he do that?"

"He came around the day after they arrested Hayden. Said he knew all about the affair my man was having—and about the words between Hayden and your daddy." Nellie took another long pull from the soda. "I told him the truth right then and there. Told him everything."

"But if Hayden was at the house that night, you couldn't have vouched for—"

"He told me what happened out at the Circle B. He was real shook when he came back. At first he wouldn't talk to me. Just poured himself a drink and sat in the chair. His hands was shaking."

Nellie's eyes stared off into the distance. It was obvious from her tone that she recalled every detail of that night. Her anguish was also apparent. Dani felt waves of compassion wash over her as the woman continued.

"After a time, he told me what he'd seen. "'Course, then we had no way of knowing that they'd pin it on him."

"They who?" Dani asked.

"The sheriff," she said with conviction. "And whoever else was in on it."

"You think the sheriff killed my parents?" Dani asked.

"I don't know who done it," Nellie admitted. "I know it wasn't Hayden. Just like I know he didn't kill hisself in that cell, like they said."

"Miss Cantrell," Dani began, her patience waning. "You're describing a pretty elaborate conspiracy. Why would someone kill my parents and Stone?"

"I don't know," Nellie answered. "But your sister believed me."

"There's more," Tyler said quietly.

He rested his hand against Dani's knee, his expression still and serious.

"More conjecture?" she asked.

"No. And Jennifer had just as many misgivings as you do now—until my mother told her what my father saw."

"And what was that? What convinced Jennifer that this grand conspiracy theory was plausible?"

"My father described what he saw in detail."

"That's right," Nellie chimed in. "He heard the shots. Saw the blood."

"Wait a minute!" Dani yelled. "My parents were stabbed, not shot."

"That's what convinced Jennifer," Tyler said as he took Dani's hands in his. "My father described everything just as it is in your dream. Jennifer realized that your nightmare was real."

Chapter Eleven

My nightmare is real! her brain screamed. Leaning back against the chair, Dani blinked once, hoping to organize her scattered thoughts.

"Hayden heard the shots," Nellie stated emphatically.

"But the coroner testified—"

"What if he was wrong?" Tyler questioned. "What if my father saw the same scene you've been calling a dream?"

"This isn't possible," she managed in a small voice. The dream played in her mind. It was all there—the flashes of light, the putrid smell of gunpowder, the blood.

Shivering, Dani rose and hugged her arms to her body. She knew he was behind her. His breath caressed the sensitive skin at her neck. The air between them held the comforting scent of his cologne.

"This is too much," she said. "Why didn't Jennifer tell me this? She could have called me in Atlanta."

"And said what?" Tyler asked. "She knew it would be tough, but she felt it was important for you to experience the nightmare again. Then the recollection would be fresh.''

The only thing fresh was the intense pain gripping her heavy heart. The whole situation seemed surreal.

''I know Hayden was telling the truth,'' Nellie insisted. ''He may have strayed a time or two, but he never lied to me.''

''Miss Cantrell,'' Dani began as she moved next to the woman, ''why didn't you go to the authorities with all this?''

Tyler stood off to one side, his hands balled in the front pockets of his jeans. A pained expression caused deep lines to appear beside his eyes. His mouth was little more than a taut line.

''Cassidy said he'd have me arrested. He said they would prove I was lying, and he'd make sure my boy was taken away and put with strangers.''

''But you could have gone to the prosecutor!'' she argued.

Nellie's back stiffened. ''I had a record. There was no way the cops was going to believe me.''

''A record?''

''I was going to pay for it,'' Nellie began. ''I was gonna pay him back as soon as I got back on my feet.''

''Pay who back?'' Dani asked, struggling yet again to follow the disjointed conversation.

''Mr. Brightwood.''

''Clayton Brightwood?''

Nellie's head bobbed up and down with verve. Several more strands from her gray chignon broke free. ''I used to work at his place. Cooking, cleaning, helping with the baby.''

"Sam?"

"It was back before his mama left. And I can't say as I blame her, not with the way Mr. Brightwood treated that poor girl."

Dani waved her hands again. "You have to tell me this in some sort of order. What does Clayton Brightwood have to do with your not coming forward?"

"He fired me for stealing money from the household accounts. I tried to tell him I was planning to pay it back, but he wouldn't listen. I know it was because of that business with the horse."

"Miss Cantrell!" Dani cried, unable to keep from sounding shocked. "You stole money to buy a horse?"

"No!" Nellie answered indignantly. "I just borrowed some cash to pay for Tyler's shots. He was just a young boy then. Needed them to get into school."

"So what does a horse have to do with any of this?"

"I saw Mr. Brightwood poison one of the horses. He added one of his toxins to the feed."

"I'm lost," she said to Tyler, imploring him with her eyes.

"Clayton's wife liked riding her horse more than she liked her husband. One day they had an argument, and she rode off," Tyler explained. "A day or so later, my mother saw Clayton put something in the horse's food. The next thing she knew, the horse convulsed and died slowly. Clayton's wife was devastated."

"That's tragic, but what does it have to do with the murder?" Dani asked.

"I told his wife what I seen," Nellie said proudly. "When she up and left him, Mr. Brightwood blamed me. Said I turned her against him. Like his cruelty had nothing to do with it."

"Okay." Dani paused, then spoke slowly. "So when Mr. Brightwood discovered the money missing, he fired you and had you arrested?"

"Right. I got convicted and had to pay restitution."

"That wouldn't have discredited you as a witness," Dani reasoned.

"Cassidy told me it would. Said no one would believe me, and I'd go to jail for perjury, or worse."

"What about later?" Dani prodded. "What about after the trial?"

"I knew someone had killed Hayden. I wasn't about to let 'em kill me, too!"

Dani looked from mother to son. It was the first time she had seen the murders from this perspective. Obviously, she wasn't the only one who'd suffered a loss. Nellie's pain was apparent from the way she sat picking nervously at her fingernails. Tyler looked like a dark cloud just waiting to explode.

"Why didn't you tell me all this after Jennifer was killed?" she asked as they were leaving the dreary home.

"I didn't think you'd believe me," he said simply.

"What makes you think I believe you now?"

He turned then, touching her with the full force of those unwavering eyes. "Because you're too smart to ignore the obvious."

"I did a pretty good job where you were concerned," she returned.

"Look, Dani," he said as he pulled out of the drive. "I didn't mean for this to get so complicated. I certainly didn't bargain on feeling something for you."

"Feeling something?"

"Have dinner with me tonight, and I'll explain it to you."

LUCKILY, it was Sandra's and Matt's night to shoot pool at the Brightwoods'. Dani was allowed to prepare for the evening without having to suffer the wrath of her aunt.

"I'll have dinner with him just so he can answer my questions," she said to her reflection as she applied a small amount of gloss to her lips.

Nellie's revelations hadn't answered as many questions as they had created. She was growing suspicious of everyone. What if Clayton Brightwood and the sheriff had conspired to kill her parents and then framed Hayden Stone?

"Two months ago, I would have laughed at the absurdity," she grumbled as she stepped into a slinky black dress with short sleeves that would cover her still-healing wound. But the visit with Nellie had been disturbing.

"But not as strange as my having dinner with Tyler," she said as she struggled into a pair of pumps. "What did he mean by feelings?"

Dani tried to ignore the flutter of anticipation in her stomach. The flutter blossomed into a hard knot when she caught her first glimpse of him. He stood in her doorway, leaning against the jamb. The jeans and casual shirt she was so accustomed to were gone, replaced by an expertly tailored gray suit of nubby raw silk. The pale suit contrasted with his deeply tanned skin and light hair. His shirt was a rich blue, as bright and vibrant as the smile he offered her.

"You look fantastic," he said in a low voice.

"Thank you," she managed to say clearly. "You clean up nice yourself."

The smile reached his eyes. He twirled his hat in his hand before placing it on his head. "All set?"

I hope so, she thought, but what she said was "Absolutely."

Tyler followed her down to the door. Dani could feel the vibration of his every step. She could smell his cologne, hear the gentle rustle of his shirtsleeves beneath his jacket. When he came up behind her and placed his hand at the small of her back, she nearly jumped out of her skin.

"Why so nervous?" he asked as they reached the car.

Dani laughed. "I would think that was obvious."

"Are you still mad at me for not telling you everything?"

She looked at him. "Probably," she answered. Even she was surprised by her response. "I'm not sure why," she admitted as he gunned the engine, "but I'm not as mad as I am curious about what happened all those years ago."

"Does this mean we're on the same side?" he asked. "Are we?"

He glanced at her for just a second. "I think so. I think you want to know the truth as much as I do."

"I suppose," she admitted. "But what will you do if you find out the worst? What if your father was the killer?"

His thumb drummed against the wheel in time to the tune playing softly on the radio. "I can accept that, Dani. Until I met with Jennifer, I thought my mother had contorted the truth to make me feel better. She always told me my father was innocent. Somewhere along the line, I allowed myself to accept the reality that she might be saying that to protect her only child from his flawed parentage."

"I know what you mean," she said. "I'm sure that's the same reason why Uncle Matt never told me about my mother's affair."

"I'm sorry if that hurt you," he said as his hand came to rest against her thigh.

Dani swallowed, trying not to notice the warmth radiating outward from his touch. It wasn't an easy task. Not when his fingers were beginning to gently knead her upper leg.

"I'm not hurt," she managed, in a deceptively controlled voice. "I told you before, I'm not an emotional cripple. My mother's infidelity didn't have anything to do with me. She was still a good mother."

"I'm glad you can separate the two."

Right then she was only concerned with separating her desires from her reason. She wondered if he had any idea of his effect on her?

The intimate restaurant he'd selected was just north of Beaumont. It was one of those shadowy places that smelled of rich cuisine and expensive wine. There were very few customers, though she immediately noticed that the place catered mostly to couples. That knowledge was somehow disconcerting.

Tyler ordered a bottle of wine while they waited for their food. She watched him by candlelight, studied his handsome features by the flickering flame.

"More?" he asked when she'd downed her first glass.

"Yes, please."

"You aren't going to do a repeat of the stunt you pulled at Carol's?"

She felt her face grow warm under his teasing eyes. "That was an accident. I hadn't had any lunch."

He nodded. "Then I'll make sure to feed you. I don't want your senses clouded. Not tonight."

"What's that supposed to mean?"

He winked, but didn't answer. Instead, he asked, "Would you like to dance?"

She looked at the deserted dance floor before nodding. What the heck? she thought. What could it hurt?

He was a graceful dancer. His motions were fluid and rhythmic. Dani had difficulty concentrating on the steps. His cologne was distracting, as was the feel of his thighs brushing hers. His arms wound around her, resting just at her waist. She flattened her palms against his chest and tried not to dwell on the rigid feel of the muscles beneath her fingers.

His eyes never left her face. She was acutely aware of his every lithe movement—and her body's instant and powerful response.

It was nothing short of a miracle that she was able to choke down her dinner. With every cell in her body tingling with anticipation, she ate without tasting. Listened without hearing.

It would have been so easy for him to continue holding her, dancing with her. It certainly seemed to Tyler like an improvement over discussing his reasons for keeping his relationship with Hayden a secret.

He studied her face, all the while wishing he could start over again. The sadness in her eyes had evolved into something more akin to trepidation.

"I really am sorry about not telling you everything," he began as the waiter placed mugs of steaming coffee in front of each of them.

He noted that her shoulders seemed to stiffen.

"I don't understand why."

He hugged the warm cup in his palms. "In the beginning, it was because I was following Jennifer's suggestions."

"And after she died?"

He looked up then, drawn by the strength he heard in her tone. It was the first time she'd mentioned her sister without her voice cracking.

She was looking at him with a kind of expectant intensity, making him feel sensations he hadn't experienced since grade school. He felt like a pupil being called on by the teacher, and he wasn't sure he had the correct answer.

"I realize now that I should have told you everything."

"Then why didn't you?" she pressed.

"I know this is going to sound pretty lame."

Her head tilted, and he saw just the hint of a smile.

"Your sister had just been killed. Then you went back to Atlanta."

"What about when I came back?"

"I was going to tell you that night I asked you to have dinner, but then my mother called."

Her expression softened fractionally, and she nodded.

"My mother had received a couple of threatening phone calls, and she begged me to stay with her for a few days."

"Did the calls have anything to do with the case?"

"Definitely," he said, leaning forward and resting his elbows against the table. "The two I listened in on were pretty ominous."

"Such as?"

"Along the lines of 'Accidents happen.' "

She raised the cup to her lips, and her eyebrows drew together in apparent thought. Still, Tyler sensed that the protective shield was still in place. She regarded him warily, caution brimming in her big, green eyes.

"My mother begged me to back off. She was afraid for my safety and for her own. I agreed, partly because it gave me a reason not to have to tell you the whole truth."

"So then what made you decide to continue investigating?" Dani asked.

"Well, once I saw how determined you were to get to the bottom of this, I knew I couldn't just walk away and leave you to face the murderer on your own," Tyler admitted. "Besides, I feel like I owe it to my father to try and clear his name."

He hoped his candor was working. It was hard to tell, because Dani had this incredible knack for concealing many of her emotions.

"If your mother was so in love with Stone, why would she object to your clearing his name?"

"She doesn't think the past can be undone. And after the calls, she got spooked."

There was a subtle change in her body language. Her shoulders appeared to relax, and she leaned forward in the seat. He prayed it was a positive sign.

"Were the calls from a man or a woman?"

"The voice was disguised, but I think it was a woman."

"A woman?" she asked in a pensive whisper.

"That's how it sounded."

"Do you have any thoughts on who it might have been?"

He shook his head and felt his shoulders slump forward.

"Maybe it was the same woman that doctored the transcripts."

"That's been nagging at me," Tyler admitted. "Who would be in a position to pull something like that off? And what makes you think it was a woman?"

"My money's on the clerk at the courthouse," she answered. "You should have seen the stricken look on her face when I asked for another copy."

"Okay." He reached out and pushed the candle off to one side. "Who could have arranged for the transcript to be altered?"

"Meyers?" she suggested. "He probably wields some power around the courthouse."

Tyler considered the suggestion briefly. "He has nothing to gain, though."

"Cassidy?"

"I think he's a likely candidate."

"But why?" she asked as her hand reached out and tapped his.

"If we assume for the moment that my father wasn't guilty, then we have to assume that he didn't kill himself, as well."

"And he was in Cassidy's custody when he was found hanged," she finished.

He noted with more than just a bit of exuberance that her tone and, most importantly, her eyes no longer held that edge of trepidation.

"And we know from what Meyers and my mother have both said that there was more information presented at the trial than we found in the transcript."

"But most of what's missing appears to be about the Cromwell deal and your father's alibi," she reasoned. "We haven't discovered anything that links Cassidy to Cromwell."

"Good point," he conceded reluctantly. "But we don't know that much about that Cromwell thing."

"Then I think," she said after a brief pause, "that's where we ought to focus our attention."

"Does this mean I'm forgiven?"

The pause lasted longer this time. "I don't like being lied to," she told him. "But I suppose I can understand how it started and why it continued. Just promise me no more lies or evasions."

"Promise," he said quickly as he reached out and placed his hand over hers. "Can we start over, Dani?"

He could almost see the thoughts churning around in her head.

"And go where?"

"How about home?"

She nodded. She also knew that her heart was affecting her brain. As she followed him out to the car, she was wondering whether it was the explanation or the man that had her teetering on the edge of forgiving him.

"Did you have a nice time?" he asked when they arrived back at the ranch.

"Very nice."

As soon as the door closed, he gathered her into his arms. Slowly, deliberately, he eased his hand up over her back, until his fingers were entwined in strands of silky brown hair. She looked up at him, her head tilted back and her lips slightly parted.

"I care about you a great deal," he said.

She said nothing, but he felt her lean into him. It was all the encouragement he needed. His mouth met hers, forceful and demanding.

With their mouths joined together, Tyler lifted her as if she were weightless, and carried her to the steps. As they neared the top, she slipped her hand inside his jacket, caressing him through the fabric. Her actions quickened his step. He entered her room and used one booted foot to close the door with a resounding thud. He sat down on her bed, with Dani draped across his lap.

"Don't go anywhere," he said against her lips as he moved away from her to shrug out of his jacket. He dropped it on the floor and placed his hands on her shoulders.

For a brief instant, he looked into her heavy-lidded, thickly lashed eyes. Finding no resistance, he pushed. She tumbled backward, and he moved with her, covering her small body with his own.

The feel of her beneath him was powerfully erotic. He reached for her wrists and caught them in his hands. Gently he moved her hands above her head. He tasted her hungrily, anxious to know every part of her.

He was only vaguely aware of her perfume. All his senses seemed to be locked on the slow gyrations of her hips. There it was again. The unexpected passion that aroused him beyond belief. He prayed for control.

Tyler tore away from her mouth and pressed his lips against the pulse point at her throat. All the while, he was attentive to keeping her hands safely above her head. A small, guttural sound escaped from her when his mouth traveled lower, kissing her through the fabric of her dress. He felt her move then, trying to free her hands.

"In a minute," he promised her as he nuzzled the valley between her firmly rounded breasts.

"Please, Tyler?"

"Not yet," he said as he bent his leg and insinuated himself between her thighs. It was his turn to moan.

With his free hand, he smoothed the few strands of hair away from her face, then made a trail from her forehead to her lower lip. He remembered vividly the night he had touched her mouth. Her tongue flicked out to moisten his fingertip, nearly sending him over the edge.

Sliding up, he again found her mouth as his hand began a slow descent over her collarbone until he felt the slope of her breast in his palm. He felt pressure as she strained against his hand and again tried to free her wrists.

"Tyler," she said urgently against his mouth.

He lifted his head and saw the fire in her green eyes. When his hand closed over her breast, Tyler watched, fascinated, as her lips parted on a sudden breath. It was a heady experience, watching her reaction as his thumb grazed her erect nipple. It pleased him immeasurably to see her reaction, to feel her response. He didn't think she was ready to admit any feeling for him, but this was enough—for now.

"I want to make love to you," he managed in a hoarse voice.

"I want that, too."

He barely allowed the final syllable before his mouth was again on hers. He teased her with his fingers. Alternating the stroke and the pressure until he began to feel her wriggle beneath him. He let go of her wrists.

Her fingers flew to his tie. Dani felt such urgency. Her heart was beating in her ears. Her skin felt hot from the exhilaration surging through her veins. Not being able to touch him had only made her more determined. Now unencumbered, she began peeling away his clothing. Tyler shifted to the side, allowing her fingers easy access to his shirt. As each button was released, she bent forward and placed a kiss against the silky hair and muscle.

When her fingers found their way to his belt buckle, Dani smiled when she heard the breath hiss through his clenched teeth. It was his turn to be the recipient of this most exquisite form of torture.

"Don't move," she said as she placed a kiss solidly on his mouth.

"Don't bet on it," he murmured as he reached for her again.

He propped himself up on his elbow and looked down at her. His shirt was shoved down to his biceps, allowing her to caress his hard, muscular arms and shoulders. The hair on his chest was much darker than the blond, disheveled mass framing his attractive face. Dani's hands moved again, and she tugged at his belt.

He responded by teasing her nipple again. A sexy half smile punctuated his expression. He slid from the bed and removed his shirt before holding his hand out to her. Dani joined him in the stream of moonlight filtering through the window.

His chest was so broad, and she marveled at the way the hair tapered across his taut stomach into a V before disappearing into his waistband. It naturally drew her attention.

"If you keep looking at me like that, I'll probably lose it again and tear your clothes off."

"No need," she said as her head tilted back. As he watched, she slowly peeled the sleeves away from her shoulders. Angling her arm behind her, Dani found the zipper and pulled it along the track at a deliberately teasing pace. The bodice fell away, revealing the edges of her lacy bra. Tyler needed no more encouragement.

He wasted no time removing her dress, tossing it on the pile with his shirt and jacket. His eyes roamed over her exposed skin. He dropped to his knees, and his open mouth fell against her stomach. She massaged the corded muscles at his shoulders while he placed warm kisses on the sensitive flesh just above her waist. Dani grabbed his head and groaned. His fingers easily released her garters before he rolled the stockings down and over her feet.

When he rose to his full height, he took Dani with him. They floated back to the bed. Tyler placed her against the pillows, then shed what remained of his clothes. She gaped in muted admiration when he stood next to her bed, devouring her with his eyes.

He moved next to her, feeling her roll against him when he joined her. He allowed himself the pleasure of looking directly into her eyes as he ran his palm over her full breasts and flat stomach. He teased her by dipping his fingertips beneath the waistband of her black lace panties. He loved watching the way her eyelids fluttered each time he explored a new area of her supple body.

As he removed her remaining garments, Tyler kissed the part of her he had uncovered. Her skin was flawlessly soft and pale beneath his hand. He could gladly have spent hours exploring every tantalizing inch of her.

"Please..." she breathed.

"Please what?" he countered as he reached to stroke the sensitive skin at the inside of her thigh.

Tyler covered her, carefully positioning himself so that he could watch her face. She caught her lower lip in her teeth when he entered her. He stopped, long enough for her to get used to him. The slow circular motion of her hips told him all he needed to know. Slipping one hand beneath her waist, he arched her against him, but made certain he could still see her expression. He watched her intently as their bodies found a primitive rhythm. He watched her eyes, her mouth, her lips.

He felt her reach for him once. Then Dani settled for massaging his chest with urgent fingers. Her eyes closed as she moved in unison with him. When she wrapped her legs around him, he found himself buried blissfully deeper. He felt her muscles begin to tense and, as she clutched him, Tyler experienced wave after wave of fierce satisfaction.

He lay next to her, cradling her in his arms. He could feel each breath against his skin and heard her contented sigh. The sound brought a purely egotistical smile to his lips.

She was curled against him, all legs and warm skin.

"There's something else," he murmured.

"What do you mean?" she purred as she traced the outline of his nipple with her fingernail.

"There's something else I haven't told you. I've wanted to do this since the first night I saw you at the airport," he said as he brushed her temple with a kiss.

Dani felt her muscles relax. She'd been holding her breath, bracing herself for some more important revelation. She placed her lips against his bared chest and drank in the scent of him.

The room wasn't completely pitch-black, and she couldn't remember the last time she had felt so contented. It felt marvelous to be in his arms, to draw on the strength of his powerful body. The past no longer mattered. Not now.

"Danielle?"

They looked up to find Sandra silhouetted in the doorway.

Chapter Twelve

Sandra backed up a step and froze in the doorway. Her hand flew to her opened mouth, and she glared at them with wide, overly made-up eyes.

"I can't believe you would do such a thing!" her aunt cried.

Self-consciously Dani tugged the edges of the comforter up to her throat. Tyler's only movement was to tighten his embrace.

"Aunt Sandra..." Dani began.

"I just can't believe this!" Sandra bellowed, waving her arms frantically in the air. "Thank God your uncle didn't see this! Did you stop long enough to think about how your behavior would affect him?"

"Aunt Sandra!"

"No! Don't speak," Sandra screeched. "Get him out of here immediately. I won't permit—"

"He's not going anywhere!" Dani told her firmly. "I'd appreciate it if you would close the door on your way out," she told her aunt pointedly.

"You've turned out to be a whore, just like your mother," Sandra said with obvious disgust before slamming the door.

"Whew!" Tyler said when they were alone.

Reaching for her robe at the end of the bed, Dani slipped from the warm covers and cursed the slight tremor in her hands.

She turned to find him beside the bed, tugging on his jeans in the shadows. She flipped on the light as she tossed her hair back over her shoulder.

"You have to get out of here," she said simply.

His easy expression clouded into a series of deep lines. "Why?"

"Why?" she repeated incredulously. "Because it isn't right—"

"What wasn't right about it?" he asked reasonably.

Dani felt flustered, and her aunt's harsh words were still stinging her ears.

"You know what I mean," she said imploringly.

"No. I don't," he said as he sat on the end of her bed.

His hair was disheveled, and very sexy. Dani lowered her eyes.

"Don't make this harder."

"I'm not doing anything," he responded. "I'm just trying to figure out why you're tossing me out."

"Because of my aunt," she admitted in a soft voice.

"You know," he said, as his hands reached back and he braced his large frame against the footboard, "I don't understand why you're letting Sandra dictate your actions."

"She raised me."

"Past tense. You're a grown woman, Dani."

"But I owe her—"

"Life is about more than paying debts," he said softly. "It's about living. It's all right for you to do what you want, not what's expected of you."

"That's absurd!"

"Really? You're so anxious to avoid confrontation that you've spent the past several years hiding in graduate school."

She gaped at him. "I'm earning my doctorate," she argued.

"To do what?"

"To...*have,*" she stammered.

"And then what? Are you going to find some other excuse to stay away from here?"

"I don't find excuses," she said with a dismissive wave of her hand.

"Jennifer told me about the succession of summer camps. The year you spent as an exchange student in high school. You're letting Sandra run you off. It's about time you stood up to her. The Circle B belongs to you."

"But they raised me, Tyler."

"So you've said thank-you. What more do you think you need to do?"

"Why are we discussing this?"

Tyler stood and walked over to her. Grasping her arms, he said, "Because you're trying to throw me out, and I don't want to go."

Tilting her head back, Dani looked into his dark eyes and felt a stirring deep within her. "I don't want you to go, either."

"That's what I'm talking about," he said as he placed a kiss on her forehead. "Being together isn't wrong, Dani, unless you let Sandra convince you that it is."

"But you heard what she said," she told him as she rested her cheek against his chest.

"I did, but did you?"

"What do you mean?" she asked, lifting her head.

"Sandra accused your mother of being a—"

"I heard."

"It sounds as if Sandra might have known about your mother and my father."

"Oh, Tyler," Dani whispered. "I know my aunt is a pain, but you can't possibly believe that she's mixed up in all this."

"We'll start digging in the morning."

Her eyes fluttered closed as she felt his hands begin a gentle exploration of her back. Tyler carried her to the bed, and their lovemaking began again, more powerful than before.

"WHERE ARE WE GOING?" she asked as they slipped out the front door before the first light of day.

"Into town."

"Why?"

"You'll see when we get there."

But she didn't. "I've already talked to Mr. Meyers. He told me everything he could remember about the trial," she said as she followed him up the walkway.

The retired prosecutor was obviously surprised by their appearance on his doorstep. A steaming mug of coffee was in one hand, the belt to his bathrobe in the other. His white hair was neatly combed, but he had not yet shaved the faint whiskers shadowing his chin.

"Miss Baylor?"

"I'm Tyler Cantrell," her companion said without preamble.

He looked from Tyler to Dani, his eyebrows severely drawn together. "Mr. Cantrell," he said, acknowledging Tyler. "I'm afraid I'm not in a position to meet with you—"

"I just need to know if you have a copy of the coroner's report from my father's trial."

Meyers did a double take, and his expression turned into one of shock. "I see you found the son," he said to Dani.

"Yes, sir."

"Come in," he said, relenting and stepping aside.

The house smelled of an inviting mixture of bacon and freshly brewed coffee.

"Thank you," she said to his back. "I'm sorry for barging in on you like this."

"You two can have some coffee while I rummage around down in the basement."

"I hope it's no trouble," she said.

Meyers just shrugged. He gave them the coffee, as promised, and then left them in the kitchen while he went in search of the file.

Dani looked at Tyler, and was unprepared for what she saw in his dark eyes.

"What's wrong?"

"I'm uncomfortable around this guy," he told her openly. "I know he was just doing his job, but if my father was innocent . . ."

Dani reached out, her fingers closing over his forearm, and gave a small squeeze. "I'm sure—"

"You two are in luck," Meyers announced upon his abrupt return. The knees of his pajamas were smudged with white dust, and he carried a tattered yellow envelope triumphantly in his hand.

"Great!" Tyler said as he extended his palm.

Meyers didn't hand the package to Tyler. Instead, he moved to the counter and carefully pulled aging papers from inside. Meyers's facial expressions varied as he scanned the pages. "Miss Baylor?" he said as he hugged the pages to his chest, "I don't think it would be advisable for you to read these."

"What are you talking about?" she asked with a trace of annoyance in her voice.

"Perhaps it would be best if Mr. Cantrell reviewed the information and the photographs."

"You have photographs?"

He nodded. "Very graphic, very unpleasant."

"He's right, Dani," Tyler said as he extracted his arm from her ever-tightening grip. "I'll look through everything in the other room."

"I can take it. Weren't you the one lecturing me on how I should stop avoiding conflict and start facing up to reality?"

"Gotta pick your spots," he said with a wink.

By the second paragraph, Tyler was glad Dani had been spared this task. The report was blunt, technical, and brutally graphic. By the time he reached the faded black-and-white pictures, a theory was taking shape in his brain.

His gut knotted when he stared down at the beautiful woman, her features frozen in death. Dani certainly resembled her mother, so much so that Tyler had to place the photo facedown on the table.

The crime scene and autopsy pictures of Milton Baylor weren't as disturbing, though they were equally telling. It wasn't until he flipped to the pictures of the living room that his theory was confirmed—at least in his mind.

After thanking Mr. Meyers, Tyler took her by the hand and escorted her from the house.

"Did you learn anything?"

"I think so," he said, hedging. "In your dream, how many shots were fired?"

Closing her eyes, Dani grimaced as she ran through the images and counted. "Five."

She opened her eyes to find him nodding.

"Here," he said as he unbuttoned his shirt and extracted two eight-by-ten pictures and handed them to her.

"You stole these?" she gasped.

"Borrowed." He shrugged. "Look at the wall behind the sofa."

Dani swallowed as she scanned the picture. She remembered the furniture, the curtains, everything. Even the sheet-draped bodies, lying beside one another on the couch.

"This dark splotch?"

"Yep," he said as he pulled the car off to the side of the main street. "The cops said the plaster was broken in a struggle, but look at the table."

"I don't understand," she admitted.

"The magazines are symmetrically laid out. That vase is full of water, and there's none on the table."

"This stuff would have been disturbed in a struggle."

"Very good," he said with a warm smile. "And that isn't a crack in the plaster," he continued. "It's too perfect, too cone-shaped."

"What does that mean?"

He hesitated just briefly before launching into his theory. "There was a clean injury to your father's left arm. I think the bullet passed through his arm and then lodged itself in the plaster. I also think that mark in the plaster was made when someone dug the slug out of the wall."

"But what about the stab wounds?"

"I think the killer did the same thing to the bodies that he did to the wall. According to the coroner's report, there were three wounds on your father, two on your mother. The same as the number of shots."

"You think they were shot, and then the killer removed the bullets?" she asked, wide-eyed. A shiver racked her small body, and revulsion left a putrid taste in her mouth.

"It makes sense, Dani."

"It's disgusting!" she said as her hand pressed against the waves of nausea churning in her stomach.

"I know this is tough," he said as his fingers gently traced the side of her face. "But we're beginning to put this together."

She nodded and took in a deep breath of fresh air. "Was there anything in the report that would implicate my aunt?" she asked.

Tyler shook his head. "It was all medical stuff."

"Now that we know the how, can we figure out the who?"

"I'm working on it," he said with a smile.

"Hi THERE!" Carol called with a cheery smile.

Dani returned her smile as she and Tyler walked toward the house. Carol eyed them with jovial suspicion.

"What brings you out here?" Dani asked.

"I thought I'd invite myself over for a cup of coffee."

Dani struggled to keep the smile on her lips. "That's nice."

"Look," Carol said as she replaced her purse on her shoulder. "If I've come at a bad time, I can always take a rain check."

"Don't be silly," Tyler insisted. Then, turning to Dani, he said, "I've got a few things to do down at the bunkhouse. I'll see to my errands, make a few calls and meet you back here in a couple of hours."

She wanted to say no, but couldn't. When she opened her mouth to speak, he placed a soft kiss on her slightly parted lips.

She met her friend's astonished eyes and felt a blush creep into her cheeks.

"See you later," he said as he bounded off the steps.

"I don't believe it!" Carol gushed as she grabbed Dani and pulled her inside the house.

"Believe what?" Dani said, feigning innocence.

Carol snorted as she marched Dani into the deserted living room. After being deposited on the couch, Dani stifled a laugh as she watched her friend scour the hallway for signs of the others.

"You did it, didn't you?"

"Did what?" Dani adopted a prim posture of neatly crossed legs and elegantly folded hands.

"C'mon, Dani," Carol said as she flung herself onto the seat. "You and Tyler . . . you did it!"

"I don't know what you're talking about," she managed to say with a guilty blush.

"You know. *It.* Set off the fireworks. Heard the music. Felt the waves crash. Played hide the—"

"Thank you," she said, interrupting her. "You're going a bit overboard."

"Tell me!" Carol pleaded. "Tell me everything. Especially the parts where he's naked."

"Will you behave?" Dani muttered, though it was hard to keep the laughter out of her voice.

"Dani, you have to tell me!" Carol insisted with a wicked smile. "I told you all about Mark Matheson."

"You were eight years old, and he paid you twenty-five cents to look up your skirt."

"So," Carol said, pretending to be offended. "It doesn't matter what happened. Best friends are supposed to tell each other all their titillating secrets."

"You've got to get out more, Carol."

"But I'm right," she announced proudly. "I can tell by your face. You and Tyler are lovers."

"Will you hush!" Dani implored.

"Why should I hush? I think it's wonderful. This is the first spontaneous thing you've done since you were six."

"I don't want to discuss it," Dani insisted.

"Then do you have pictures?" Carol said as she wickedly rubbed her hands together in an excited fashion.

"That's perverted!"

"Okay." Carol relented, tucking one leg beneath her slender frame. "If you won't tell the details, at least tell me how this happened."

"Who said anything happened?"

"Right, Dani," Carol quipped. "He kept his hands on you from the moment you got out of the car. Then there was that romantic little peck on the lips. He told you exactly what he'd be doing and when he'd be back. Those are the early signs of true love."

"Stop it," Dani said as she dissolved into giggles. "We're getting acquainted. That's all."

"My foot! I think it's great. You need someone like Tyler to add some spice to your dreary life."

"My life is *not* dreary."

"Oh, nooo," Carol teased. "You've written me scores of letters in the past few years. I can chronicle your existence in three words. Study, research, write. Study, research, write."

"That's six words," Dani said defensively as she offered her tongue.

"Repeats don't count. And then you come back and have a mad, passionate fling with your ranch foreman."

"Calm yourself, Carol," Dani instructed. Lowering her voice, she continued, "He also happens to be Hayden Stone's son."

"I'll be damned!" Carol said through her obvious shock.

Dani rose and checked the hallway again. Finding it clear, she rejoined her friend. "It's crazy, I know."

"Not really," Carol offered hopefully. "It has been twenty years, and he can't be held responsible for what his father did."

"I know."

Carol's pretty features hardened with apparent concentration. "Is this going to be a problem for you two?"

"You're acting as if there is something permanent happening between Tyler and me."

"If a man looked at me that way, I'd certainly hope it was permanent."

"What are you two doing hiding in the living room?" Sandra asked them.

"We aren't hiding," Dani said as she stared into her aunt's icy blue eyes. "We were just talking."

"Where is Tyler? Buck was looking for him. I assume he's still working for us?"

One eyebrow arched above Sandra's eye, nearing the mound of teased hair fluffed around her forehead. Her nails and lips were bright red, as were her oversize blouse and spandex pants.

"He'll be back in a while," Dani answered.

"You had a phone call this morning," Sandra said with obvious annoyance. "It was from some laboratory."

"Hilland Labs?" Dani prompted, recalling her recent donation of blood.

Sandra nodded. "They said their findings were positive for chloroethyl alcohol."

Dani rushed toward the taller woman, her fingers biting into the flesh of her upper arm. "Are you sure, Aunt Sandra?"

Shrugging away, Sandra smoothed the wrinkles in her blouse and leveled her eyes on Dani. Casually, brazenly, she said, "If you wanted to know what I used, all you had to do was ask."

Chapter Thirteen

"Are you saying *you* used the chloroethyl alcohol?" Dani managed through her astonishment.

Sandra appeared taken aback by her tone. Her face contorted into a series of lines and frowns. "Of course I used the polish," she answered.

Carol appeared by her side, and Dani was silently grateful for the support. She'd always known her aunt to be thoughtless and selfish, but she never would have expected the woman to so callously admit that she'd been the one to poison the rag.

"Clayton showed me how to get those nice, even strokes. Why, you can see every lustrous grain of wood."

"What wood?" Dani stammered.

"The breakfront!" Sandra said impatiently. Brushing past them, she made her way through the living room and into the dining room, where she ran her hand across the glossy top of the piece. "You'd never know it was more than a century old," Sandra said, gleaming proudly.

Dani, with Carol on her heels, followed the vaporous trail of her aunt's perfume into the adjoining room. "You're talking about *this?*"

Sandra's hands rested against her hips. "Well, what are you talking about?" she countered. "You could have just asked me about my work. You didn't need to have some lab tell you what was used." Sandra's lips curled down in a frown. "And you didn't scratch the finish, did you?"

While her aunt crouched to inspect the glazed top, Carol squeezed her arm.

"What's this all about?" her friend whispered against her ear.

"I'll tell you later," she answered. Then, in a louder voice, she asked her aunt, "And you say Mr. Brightwood was the one who gave you the polish?"

"Why this sudden interest in restoration?" Sandra asked wearily.

"I'm just very impressed by your work, Aunt Sandra."

The tactic worked. Sandra was always willing to talk about her favorite subject—anything having to do with herself.

"Clayton has been restoring old pieces for decades. You should see his home. He has this marvelous work space behind his house. Every conceivable tool, paint, polish and preservative known to mankind."

"Do you think you could take me there to see it?" Dani asked with a forced smile.

Her aunt's expression blossomed under the perceived compliment. "Why, of course," she said. "I have a key to the shop."

"Do you think we could go now?" Dani asked.

"You mean, *right* now?" Sandra asked.

"I'm very interested," Dani insisted as she looped her arm through Sandra's. "I'd love to see how you managed to turn this old relic into such a showpiece."

"That's a little thick," Carol said against her ear.

Dani swatted at her friend and steered her aunt toward the car door. "Carol, would you be a dear and tell Tyler I've gone to the Brightwoods'?"

"Sure," her friend said, in a soft, confused voice.

"How many pieces has Clayton helped you restore?" Dani asked as she started the car.

"The breakfront is my first major work. I'm about to tackle the wardrobe in Jennifer's room. The one you carved your initials in when you were ten."

Dani swallowed nervously. "Sorry."

"Yes, well, it was typical of your destructive behavior."

"Speaking of which," Dani said as she nervously cleared her throat, "you made a remark about my mother last night."

She could see her aunt stiffen against the seat in her peripheral vision. "I can't believe you would entertain a man in your room, under my roof."

It isn't your roof, she thought as irritation edged its way along her spine. "I'm sorry if that bothered you," Dani managed to say tightly.

"Of course it would bother me!" she bellowed. "I don't think that sort of behavior is appropriate. But, given your lineage, perhaps it is inevitable."

"I know about my mother's affair," Dani said firmly. She heard the small gasp of surprise from the other woman, and had to stifle a satisfied smirk.

"I see."

"I don't think you do," Dani announced. "I won't tolerate you making unflattering references about my mother."

"You won't tolerate?" Sandra said huffily.

"No, I won't."

"I think you're forgetting yourself, Danielle."

"No," Dani said with a sad smile. "I think I'm just finding myself. I own the Circle B now."

"Not all of it."

"Enough to start making some of the rules."

"Where is your gratitude?" Sandra wailed.

"I've been grateful for twenty years," she answered calmly. "I will not put up with you calling my mother names, and presuming to tell me what I can and cannot do."

"He's responsible for this, isn't he?" Sandra said in an accusing tone.

"If you are talking about Tyler, the answer is no."

"Your uncle and I gave up everything for you and your sister."

"I know that, Aunt Sandra. But somewhere along the line I allowed you to control my life. I'm just letting you know that things are about to change."

Dani turned off the highway when she saw the massive iron gates of the Brightwood spread.

"I cannot believe you would be this cruel to me, especially since you know about the affair."

Dani chanced a look in her aunt's direction. She looked like a small child pouting through a reprimand. "I don't think one has anything to do with the other."

She drove around the side of the house toward a collection of outbuildings.

"Why, that's absurd!" Sandra bellowed defensively. "You're an adult now. Surely you can imagine what it was like for me. Having to look at you. Care for you. Pretend it didn't matter."

"Back up," Dani instructed as she braked and tossed the gearshift into neutral. Turning in the seat, she was about to voice her question, when she saw the shocked expression on her aunt's face.

Following the older woman's wide-eyed stare, she looked over her shoulder, right into the barrel of a gun.

Chapter Fourteen

"Get out of the car!" Clayton commanded.

Dani was only vaguely aware of her actions. With her eyes fixed on the weapon, she numbly followed the instructions.

"Clayton," she heard her aunt say, "is this wise?"

"Necessary," the burly rancher answered. The gun jiggled slightly in his grip. "I was right about Cantrell. He's Nellie's bastard."

Sandra appeared at the man's side, her eyes full of venom, but tempered by what Dani hoped was reason.

Glancing around, her mind working furiously, Dani searched for a means of escape. The ranch was deserted.

"What are we going to do?" Sandra asked.

"Get on into the shop, Danielle," he said with a pointed wave of the gun.

She leaned back against the car and hesitated. "Mr. Brightwood, I don't know what the problem is, but—"

"Inside!" he barked.

The adrenaline surging through her system produced a near-deafening drumming in her ears. She was scared, shocked, and trying desperately to keep from giving in to the panic smothering her senses.

She went first, her step quickened by the gentle nudge of the gun barrel at the small of her back. Her hand shook as she reached for the door latch and gave a tug.

Once inside, she heard one of them bolt the door. The strong smell of chemicals joined with the unmistakable scent of fear as she cowered against a sawdust-covered workbench.

Clayton kept the gun level, trained in her direction. Sandra stood at his side, her hands clasped, her expression stiff.

"I always wondered if I'd get the chance to get even with you for what you did to my boy," Clayton began.

"That was a long time ago," Dani immediately responded.

"You damn near ruined his life with your accusations," the man thundered. "He still has a hard time in this community. Folks don't forget that easy."

"I would be happy to publicly apologize for anything—"

He cut in. "That time's come and gone."

"But what about Cantrell?" Sandra injected. Her hand went to the beefy man's arm. "Are you going to hold her here? Use her to lure him?"

Clayton laughed. "We're beyond that. She knows, Sandra."

"I don't know anything!" Dani insisted. "I don't even know what you're talking about."

"I think she's telling the truth," Sandra said.

"Well, that's too bad," Clayton said, without any real regret to back up the words. "Now it's too late."

"You can't do this!" Sandra cried desperately.

Dani was shocked by her aunt's defense, and grateful for it.

"Matt would never accept it."

"Do you think he'd rather go to jail?" Clayton asked sardonically.

"Why would Uncle Matt go to jail?" Dani asked.

A slow, taunting smile curved the man's lips. "For murder," he said with perverse pleasure.

"Uncle Matt?" she yelped.

"I told you she didn't know," Sandra cackled.

"Yes, Danielle. Matthew is the killer you and Cantrell have been chasing all over the county."

Dani felt her knees buckle, and she reached behind her for support. "That's crazy," she managed to whisper. "You're the one holding a gun on me. Uncle Matt isn't—"

"How do you think I knew to expect you?" Clayton asked.

"But I don't understand!" she said, clearly dazed and confused. "It can't be true."

"It wasn't his fault," Sandra began. "If your mother hadn't flaunted her affair with Hayden Stone in Matt's face, he would have been thinking more clearly."

"Why would that have made a difference?" she asked.

Sandra's head tilted to one side, and she stared at Dani for several seconds before speaking. "I thought you just said you knew about the affair."

"With Hayden Stone."

Her aunt's head dipped slightly as a few low, mirthless laughs gurgled from her throat. "Not with Stone. With Matthew."

"Oh, God," Dani whispered as so many pieces of her puzzling childhood fell into place. "Is Uncle Matt my father?" she managed to ask in a small voice.

"He always liked to think so," Sandra said disgustedly. "But no, he isn't your father."

"Why do you think he killed my parents?" she asked.

"Good heavens, Dani! I was there!"

With her thoughts swimming against the current of her fear, Dani found it hard to digest this terrible story. *Not Uncle Matt!* her mind screamed.

"Thanks to your mother's double-crossing, Cromwell dropped the project," Clayton said through a sneer. "We have to make some decisions," he said to Sandra.

"We can't hurt her. Matt won't stand for it."

"Would he rather stand trial?" Clayton retorted. "Or how about you? We'll all go to jail."

"Why will you go to jail?" Dani asked Clayton.

His expression lingered somewhere between menace and boredom. He sucked in a breath before saying, "Matt lost it after the shooting. Sandra called me, and I cleaned the place up. Told them what to do. It was my idea to use Stone's knife to retrieve the bullets. He and your father fought that day about the

Cromwell development. Somehow Stone found out that Matt was negotiating with the developer to sell off the ranch.''

"I'm telling you, Clayton, Matt has a soft spot for this one. It won't be like it was with Stone or Jennifer."

"Aunt Sandra, no!" Dani cried.

"She made the same mistake you did," Clayton explained. "She couldn't leave the past buried. We didn't have a choice."

It took a split second for Dani's brain to register a flash of movement just outside the window. *Think,* her mind yelled. *Buy time.*

"Jen found out Uncle Matt killed my parents?"

"Yep," Clayton said as he shifted his weight. The gun remained steady.

"And Uncle Matt and you," she said slowly, leveling her eyes on Sandra, "killed her?"

She desperately wanted to turn her head, to look for confirmation that someone was actually outside. She didn't dare. She didn't even allow her eyes to flutter in the direction of the window, for fear of alerting them.

"None of this would have happened if your father would have agreed to sell," Sandra said defensively, as if that justified the killings. "Your mother promised to persuade him to change his mind."

"And she couldn't?"

"Didn't is more like it," Sandra said with a huff. "She let Matthew believe that she was on his side, when all the time she was feeding Stone the same lines."

"If Uncle Matt was betrayed by my mother, why did he kill my father, too?"

"He panicked," Clayton said simply. "Your father wasn't supposed to come back that night, so when he showed up and caught Matt by surprise, he shot him, too."

"So they *were* shot?" Dani murmured.

"That was stupid!" Clayton bellowed. "He even used his own damned gun!"

"But why would you frame Stone?"

Clayton's smile was slow and sinister. "My idea. Why? I always hated that arrogant fool. Cassidy hated him, too, so that made it simple."

"And the sheriff?" Dani continued, her hopes waning, as time and the large man's interest appeared to be growing thin.

"It cost us a few dollars, but Cassidy was willing to cooperate. He probably enjoyed killing Stone." The rancher tilted his hat back on his forehead and let out a loud, exasperated breath. "I'm getting tired of your questions."

"But we can't just kill her," Sandra insisted. "How can I explain another death in my family?"

"Matthew's taking care of that. We'll all say she was distraught over Jennifer's accident."

"But what about Tyler?"

No sooner had her aunt said his name than the door burst open on a gust of wind and splintering wood.

Dani barely had time to breathe before she felt herself being propelled across the table under a crushing weight. She heard the sounds of a scuffle. There were shouts and screams, followed by the distant whine of sirens.

"Are you all right?"

"Tyler!" she gushed as soon as he peeled himself off her.

He pulled her up and steadied her with his hands. It was only then that she caught her first sight of Sam holding a rifle.

"She okay?"

"Yep," Tyler said to the younger Brightwood.

"Think about what you're doing," Clayton instructed his son.

"I am," Sam said sadly. He made no move to lower his weapon.

Sandra and Clayton were crouched in the corner, with Sam standing guard a few feet away. The sirens grew closer, until Dani could feel the shrill sound through a vibration in the floor.

She looked up into Tyler's eyes and felt her heart begin to swell and grow heavy. His hands gently cupped her face, his thumbs gently stroking the stream of tears spilling from her eyes.

"I know what happened," she said with a gulp. "Your father wasn't the one."

Suddenly the shop filled with armed state troopers clad in bulletproof vests.

"Hush," he said as he gathered her to him. "All that matters to me is that you're safe."

"THIS IS BEAUTIFUL," she cried, tossing her case on the floor and throwing open a window.

"No," Tyler said, slipping his hands around her waist and locking his fingers against her fluttering stomach. "You are beautiful."

"Thank you," she said softly. She stood silently admiring their reflection in the mirror above the dresser. "What happens now?"

"You get to select the tacky Vegas chapel of your choice and marry me."

She smiled and felt her heart fill with emotion. "Since you asked me to marry you in the middle of total chaos, I'll understand if you decide to give it some more thought."

He turned her in his arms. "I love you, Dani. I know that. We may have been brought together by the worst possible circumstances, but I'm sure of how I feel."

"Me too," she admitted with a small smile. "I guess I'm just not quite used to all this spontaneity."

His kiss was gentle, loving.

"What do you think will happen to Sandra and Matt?" she asked as he cradled her in his arms.

"I hear Sandra is turning on all of them, trying to cut a deal. I guess her attorney's going to claim that she was some sort of victim in all this."

"She didn't appear too victimized when she and Clayton were holding me at gunpoint."

She felt his grip tighten.

"I have never felt as helpless as I did when Sam and I were standing outside the workshop."

"It's over," she said softly.

"But when I think of what might have happened . . ."

"We're both safe," she reminded him.

"Thanks to Sam."

"I guess he isn't the saber-toothed creep I thought he was."

"Everyone makes mistakes," Tyler reasoned. "Lying to you was the biggest mistake *I* ever made."

"That's behind us," she told him.

"But there's still some rough going ahead of us."

"The trial?" she asked.

"Trials," he said. "They'll try Cassidy separately for killing my father."

"What about after this is over?" she asked as she stepped back.

He looked down at her upturned face. "I think that's the part where we get to live happily ever after."

She smiled at him and said, "I know that part. I'm talking about logistics. We haven't talked about the ranch."

"What's there to talk about?" he countered as his fingers traced the edge of her cheekbone. "I love the Circle B."

"But when we get right down to it, the ranch has cost us both dearly."

"Do you want to walk away from it?"

"No," she answered quickly. It was his turn to smile. "The Circle B is our home. But I would understand if you wanted to get rid of it," she promised.

His fingers wound into the silky strands of her hair. "I don't want you to sell the Circle B. As far as I'm concerned, we only have one issue to settle."

"What?"

"You still have to pick a chapel."

Just before he kissed her lips, Tyler noticed that the sadness was finally gone from Dani's eyes.

HARLEQUIN®

I N T R I G U E®

Harlequin Intrigue
invites you to
celebrate

It's a year of celebration for Harlequin Intrigue, as we commemorate ten years of bringing you the best in romantic suspense. Stories in which you can expect the unexpected... Stories that walk the fine line between danger and desire...

And to help celebrate, you can RETURN TO THE SCENE OF THE CRIME with a limited hardcover collection of four of Harlequin Intrigue's most popular earlier titles, written by four of your favorite authors:

REBECCA YORK	Shattered Vows
	(43 Light Street novel)
M.J. RODGERS	For Love or Money
PATRICIA ROSEMOOR	Crimson Holiday
LAURA PENDER	Déjà Vu

This unique collection will not be available in retail stores and is only available through this exclusive offer.

MILLION DOLLAR SWEEPSTAKES (III)

HARLEQUIN®

I N T R I G U E®

COMING NEXT MONTH

#297 EDGE OF ETERNITY by Jasmine Cresswell
Weddings, Inc.

Recluse David Powell got the unlikeliest guest at his isolated lighthouse hideaway—his ex-wife, Eve. Hell-bent on a tell-all exposé, Eve probed too deeply into David's hermitage, and now someone wanted her stopped. Was it David, the man she'd never stopped loving?

#298 TALONS OF THE FALCON by Rebecca York
Peregrine Connection #1

She'd once been in his heart, now psychologist Eden Sommers had to get into Lieutenant Colonel Mark Bradley's head. Helping him recover his memory of a top secret mission might bring back the lover she'd once known, but it might cost him his life....

#299 PRIVATE EYES by Madeline St. Claire
Woman of Mystery

P.I. Lauren Pierce was none too happy about having to hire a competing P.I. as a lookout—especially when Bill Donelan seemed to watch more than her back. But then Lauren's client turned up dead, and she became the next target....

#300 GUILTY AS SIN by Cathy Gillen Thacker
Legal Thriller

All the evidence said that wealthy, powerful Jake Lockhart was guilty of murder in the first degree. Only his attorney was convinced of his innocence. Susan Kilpatrick was sure Jake had secret information that could set him free. More than the trial was at stake if she was wrong—so was her life.

AVAILABLE THIS MONTH:

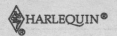 HARLEQUIN®  Silhouette®

The movie event of the season can be the reading event of the year!

Lights... The lights go on in October when CBS presents Harlequin/Silhouette Sunday Matinee Movies. These four movies are based on bestselling Harlequin and Silhouette novels.

Camera... As the cameras roll, be the first to read the original novels the movies are based on!

Action... Through this offer, you can have these books sent directly to you! Just fill in the order form below and you could be reading the books...before the movie!

48288-4	Treacherous Beauties by Cheryl Emerson		
		$3.99 U.S./$4.50 CAN.	☐
83305-9	Fantasy Man by Sharon Green		
		$3.99 U.S./$4.50 CAN.	☐
48289-2	A Change of Place by Tracy Sinclair		
		$3.99 U.S./$4.50CAN.	☐
83306-7	Another Woman by Margot Dalton		
		$3.99 U.S./$4.50 CAN.	☐

TOTAL AMOUNT	$	
POSTAGE & HANDLING	$	
($1.00 for one book, 50¢ for each additional)		
APPLICABLE TAXES*	$	_____
TOTAL PAYABLE	$	_____
(check or money order—please do not send cash)		

To order, complete this form and send it, along with a check or money order for the total above, payable to Harlequin Books, to: **In the U.S.:** 3010 Walden Avenue, P.O. Box 9047, Buffalo, NY 14269-9047; **In Canada:** P.O. Box 613, Fort Erie, Ontario, L2A 5X3.

Name: _____

Address: _____ City: _____

State/Prov.: _____ Zip/Postal Code: _____

*New York residents remit applicable sales taxes.
 Canadian residents remit applicable GST and provincial taxes.

CBSPR

"HOORAY FOR HOLLYWOOD" SWEEPSTAKES

HERE'S HOW THE SWEEPSTAKES WORKS

OFFICIAL RULES — NO PURCHASE NECESSARY

To enter, complete an Official Entry Form or hand print on a 3" x 5" card the words "HOORAY FOR HOLLYWOOD", your name and address and mail your entry in the pre-addressed envelope (if provided) or to: "Hooray for Hollywood" Sweepstakes, P.O. Box 9076, Buffalo, NY 14269-9076 or "Hooray for Hollywood" Sweepstakes, P.O. Box 637, Fort Erie, Ontario L2A 5X3. Entries must be sent via First Class Mail and be received no later than 12/31/94. No liability is assumed for lost, late or misdirected mail.

Winners will be selected in random drawings to be conducted no later than January 31, 1995 from all eligible entries received.

Grand Prize: A 7-day/6-night trip for 2 to Los Angeles, CA including round trip air transportation from commercial airport nearest winner's residence, accommodations at the Regent Beverly Wilshire Hotel, free rental car, and $1,000 spending money. (Approximate prize value which will vary dependent upon winner's residence: $5,400.00 U.S.); 500 Second Prizes: A pair of "Hollywood Star" sunglasses (prize value: $9.95 U.S. each). Winner selection is under the supervision of D.L. Blair, Inc., an independent judging organization, whose decisions are final. Grand Prize travelers must sign and return a release of liability prior to traveling. Trip must be taken by 2/1/06 and is subject to airline schedules and accommodations availability.

Sweepstakes offer is open to residents of the U.S. (except Puerto Rico) and Canada who are 18 years of age or older, except employees and immediate family members of Harlequin Enterprises, Ltd., its affiliates, subsidiaries, and all agencies, entities or persons connected with the use, marketing or conduct of this sweepstakes. All federal, state, provincial, municipal and local laws apply. Offer void wherever prohibited by law. Taxes and/or duties are the sole responsibility of the winners. Any litigation within the province of Quebec respecting the conduct and awarding of prizes may be submitted to the Regie des loteries et courses du Quebec. All prizes will be awarded; winners will be notified by mail. No substitution of prizes are permitted. Odds of winning are dependent upon the number of eligible entries received.

Potential grand prize winner must sign and return an Affidavit of Eligibility within 30 days of notification. In the event of non-compliance within this time period, prize may be awarded to an alternate winner. Prize notification returned as undeliverable may result in the awarding of prize to an alternate winner. By acceptance of their prize, winners consent to use of their names, photographs, or likenesses for purpose of advertising, trade and promotion on behalf of Harlequin Enterprises, Ltd., without further compensation unless prohibited by law. A Canadian winner must correctly answer an arithmetical skill-testing question in order to be awarded the prize.

For a list of winners (available after 2/28/95), send a separate stamped, self-addressed envelope to: Hooray for Hollywood Sweepstakes 3252 Winners, P.O. Box 4200, Blair, NE 68009.

CBSRLS

OFFICIAL ENTRY COUPON

"Hooray for Hollywood"
SWEEPSTAKES!

Yes, I'd love to win the Grand Prize — a vacation in Hollywood — or one of 500 pairs of "sunglasses of the stars"! Please enter me in the sweepstakes!

This entry must be received by December 31, 1994.
Winners will be notified by January 31, 1995.

Name _____

Address _____ Apt. _____

City _____

State/Prov. _____ Zip/Postal Code _____

Daytime phone number _____
(area code)

Mail all entries to: Hooray for Hollywood Sweepstakes,
P.O. Box 9076, Buffalo, NY 14269-9076.
In Canada, mail to: Hooray for Hollywood Sweepstakes,
P.O. Box 637, Fort Erie, ON L2A 5X3.

KCH

OFFICIAL ENTRY COUPON

"Hooray for Hollywood"
SWEEPSTAKES!

Yes, I'd love to win the Grand Prize — a vacation in Hollywood — or one of 500 pairs of "sunglasses of the stars"! Please enter me in the sweepstakes!

This entry must be received by December 31, 1994.
Winners will be notified by January 31, 1995.

Name _____

Address _____ Apt. _____

City _____

State/Prov. _____ Zip/Postal Code _____

Daytime phone number _____
(area code)

Mail all entries to: Hooray for Hollywood Sweepstakes,
P.O. Box 9076, Buffalo, NY 14269-9076.
In Canada, mail to: Hooray for Hollywood Sweepstakes,
P.O. Box 637, Fort Erie, ON L2A 5X3.

KCH